REJECTED DRAGON

ETERNITY SHIFTERS - BOOK FIVE

LOLA GABRIEL

Rejected Dragon:
Eternity Shifters - Book Five

First printing, 2022

Publisher

Secret Woods Books
secretwoodsbooks@gmail.com
www.SecretWoodsBooks.com

SECRET WOODS BOOKS

Receive a FREE paranormal romance eBook by visiting our website and signing up for our mailing list:

SecretWoodsBooks.com

By signing up for our mailing list, you'll receive a FREE paranormal romance eBook. The newsletter will also provide information on upcoming books and special offers.

1

GISELA

The party had barely started, and I already wanted it to be over. Actually, I never wanted it, period, or the reason behind it—my impending marriage to our pack's Alpha, Xander.

I sipped my shifter mead, wishing the floor of this tavern would swallow me up and teleport me somewhere else. Even though I tried to stay tucked out of everyone's way, their eyes drifted over to me. If they weren't looking my way, then they were doing a terrible job of pretending I wasn't the center of all the gossip.

They were all asking the same thing: *Why did Xander have to pick her?*

I asked myself the same question every day, but more out of quiet despair than anything else.

A woman from my pack bumped me, "accidentally," making me spill some of my drink on my shirt. She didn't apologize or turn back to look at what she had done. I didn't expect any courtesy, anyway.

"Hey, watch it!" my best friend Hailey called after the woman. Then, she examined my shirt. "Come on, I think we can get the stain out if we hurry."

She led me to the bathroom, which was thankfully empty. I gathered paper towels and dampened them, dabbing at the splash of mead on the plain gray fabric of my blouse. My mother had chastised me for wearing something so plain to the party, as if my wardrobe was made up of anything flashy. I already got enough unwanted male attention in my boring wardrobe of neutrals and jeans.

"Ugh, she's such an asshole," Hailey said, leaning against the wall of the bathroom.

"Maybe I'll be treated differently after...you know." I couldn't say the word. The thought of my wedding made me queasy.

"Or not. They're all jealous, and once you've been locked in with Xander, it'll only get worse. Or more underhanded." Hailey sighed, putting her thick black curls up into a bun. Unlike me, she wore bright colors that accentuated her dark hair and skin well, making her stand out like a beacon in the bar. If she wasn't my best friend, I'd be more jealous of her style.

"I can't believe anyone would be jealous of me having Xander," I said. "Are they that blinded by his Alpha status? Is everyone else seeing a different man than I am?"

"Yup. Case in point, your entire family."

I ran my hands down my face in frustration. My parents and older brother loved Xander. Or rather, they loved all the perks they got from being the family of the Alpha's soon-to-be wife—money, status, more influence in the pack. They were outside kissing his ass and hanging on his every word as if he ever had anything interesting to say.

Two women came in, which was our cue to leave. We went into the main room of the tavern, finding our previous spot taken. I saw another empty spot away from others, but it meant walking past several tables. Not ideal, but it was better than standing around and having people stare.

"I need another drink," Zach, a dragon shifter around our age, said to Hailey as if she were a waitress. Then again, all of the males in our pack assumed females only existed to serve them.

"Bite me," she replied, a tinge of laughter in her voice. "Get it yourself."

"Show some respect," he snarled.

My heart pounded out of my chest. Hailey was an orphan and didn't have a family reputation to maintain. That landed us in situations like this more than I wanted to count—moments away from starting some conflict.

"I'll get you something," Tammy, another dragon shifter at the table behind Zach, said. She stood, her eyes going up and down our bodies with disdain. "I don't mind at all."

"Have fun with that," Hailey said, walking on.

"I swear, Hailey," I said, shaking my head.

She raised an eyebrow at me, giving me a look that she didn't need to clarify. It said, *speak up, Gisela,* something she'd told me time and time again. Easy for her to say. No one smacked her down if she dared to express her own opinion.

"We can always go through with the plan," she said, standing up against the wall in the corner we'd chosen. "Then we wouldn't have to worry about these things."

The plan wasn't solid. It was more of a mashup of wishful thinking and recklessness. The likelihood of us leaving our pack and finding somewhere else to live out the rest of our lives was so slim that it was almost laughable. Our meager savings wouldn't get us far.

"Gisela!" Xander shouted across the room. The entire room hushed. "Come here."

I wasn't going to disobey him in front of the entire pack, so I did as he said. Xander was seated on the opposite side of the room, in a big, throne-like chair. My brother, Geoffrey, and my father were seated closer to him, my mother in the background as she always was. Hailey followed, but the moment my father saw her, he sneered.

"Leave, Hailey," Dad said. "You're not needed."

Hailey narrowed her eyes, pausing, before deciding against an act of rebellion. Acting against an older male shifter in the Alpha's presence was a recipe for harsh punishment. She turned and left.

"Sit." Xander gestured to his knee.

It was the last place I wanted to sit, but what choice did I have? I perched on his leg, but he yanked me toward him, so my body was pressed against his. Then he ran his hand up my back until it was around the nape of my neck. The aggressive nature of his touch made me think he wanted to stop me from getting away.

I winced but tried to play it off. He was possessive because I was an object to him, not because he loved and treasured me. A pretty doll to sit there with her mouth shut. Xander kept his hand on the back of my neck as he continued his conversation with my father and brother, who had hardly given me a second glance.

"The pack really is growing," Geoffrey said. "At least five new babies are coming this year."

The influx of babies was unusual for sure. Magical beings could have children, but it was a rarity, often taking hundreds of years to happen for most couples. The part of me who loved babies and had always wanted one rejoiced, but then reality smacked it down. The thought of having Xander's baby was worse than any nightmare I'd ever had.

"It's great," Dad said. "We'll need more space soon. That'll be difficult, especially these days."

"I know. Trust me, I have plans to remedy that. We have the right to take what's ours." Xander ran his thumb across the back of my neck, sending chills down my spine. "I hope that Gisela can carry on my bloodline. Sooner rather than later."

I stiffened. No amount of self-control would have stopped me from doing it. I'd put off thoughts of our wedding night even more than I'd pushed away thoughts of marrying Xander. I was a virgin, as my family and the entire pack expected of young female dragon shifters, and I had the feeling that Xander wasn't going to be the gentle lover that I had always wanted for my first time.

And now he wanted to get me pregnant right away? The entire idea of this marriage got worse and worse. Had he chosen me because my mother was so fertile? What if the baby was a girl? Was she doomed to the same restrictive fate that I was stuck in? Was Xander even going to be a good father? I highly doubted it.

Xander's grip on the back of my neck tightened. Of course he noticed the change in my body language. My family looked to me for a reaction, and I finally remembered to wipe the horror from my face. I plastered on a smile.

"I would love a baby," I said.

Xander's hand gradually relaxed, but I didn't. He never forgot a single misstep I made.

The males continued their conversation, discussing plans for a pack party after the wedding and some territory scuffles with the dragon shifter pack to the east of us. I zoned out, the tight smile never leaving my face. This was hell. My long, long life was going to be like this day after day—no freedom, no tenderness, no love.

My mother came to mind. Her entire relationship with my dad was him barking orders to her, then her either doing them or delegating them to me. I would have had some empathy for her if she didn't use every opportunity to remind me that I was a burden, and she could hardly stand for me to be in her presence.

Geoffrey was on the same path. He wasn't married yet, but he was probably going to find a wife who served him the most, not the woman he genuinely loved. Was he even capable of genuine love? It was an honest question.

These people were my family, but they were strangers to me. I wouldn't have chosen them, or even certain aspects of their personality, if I could. Guilt rushed up in me. Hailey's parents had been killed in an accident when she was twelve, and she didn't have anyone anymore. I had family, and I hated them.

And they clearly hated me. My mother never touched me with kindness—she only beat me whenever I tried to assert myself or dared to have a thought of my own. Same with my father. And my brother never hit me, but his cutting words and insults did their own kind of damage. He had been nothing but a bully to me.

Now, though, I was useful to them, so they did a good job at faking politeness toward me. Was that all I was to people? A person to use and get use from? Xander wasn't going to try to get to know me. I was exchanging one shitty family for an even worse one. And if we had a child, that child would be just as trapped as I was.

My breathing picked up, and a panic attack loomed in the corners of my consciousness.

"Excuse me, Alpha?" I asked in a demure voice when there was a break in the conversation. "May I be excused to use the restroom?"

"Sure." He nudged me off his lap with more force than I was expecting, propelling me forward.

I went toward the bathroom but walked past it and went out the back door. The tavern's air was too thick to breathe, and I didn't want anyone to see me break down.

I sucked in deep breaths when I got outside, trying to keep them even so I wouldn't fly into a full-blown panic attack. An overturned box was close to the door, which I sat on, resting my elbows on my knees and my face in my hands. When I cried, it showed on my face for hours, so I tried my hardest to keep it in.

Just when I thought I had it under control, the door flew open, banging against the wall.

"What are you doing?" Xander asked, stalking toward me. I flinched, but he cut in before I could speak. "Why did you lie to me and say you were going to the bathroom? What were you doing out here? Was there another man out here?"

"N-no. I wasn't doing anything. I felt a little bit overwhelmed by the noise of the party, and someone needed the stall. I've been out here alone," I said, the lie rolling off my lips with surprising ease. Was it really that big of a deal? The bathroom was down the hall, and he hadn't told me to come right back.

Regardless, he didn't accept my excuse. His gray eyes flashed with rage, and he grabbed me by the arm, yanking me to my feet. I cried out—his fingers were going to leave a bruise for sure. I was hundreds of times stronger than a human woman, but that didn't mean a thing against a massive male dragon Alpha.

"Listen, Gisela," he growled, pushing me against the wall by my shoulder, knocking the breath out of me. He towered over me, blocking out my entire field of vision. "I'm marrying you because you're pure. If a man even looks at you the wrong way, I'll fight him. You're mine. So don't tempt any men."

I blinked and nodded. Had I not just said that there weren't any men around? Xander's jealousy was a thing of nightmares, and I knew he wasn't messing around when he said he'd fight a man who looked at me too long. Gods, I already did my best to blend in. How much more could I do? Was I going to be responsible for some guy getting his face punched in?

And worse, Xander would definitely blame me for "tempting" a man and punish me as well.

"I'll let you off easy this time because I'm nice," he said, unaware of the terror pulsing through my veins. "But you'll officially be my property soon, and I don't take kindly to lies. I can make your life a living hell. Understood?"

I nodded, gasping for breath. He scanned my expression for a moment before letting me go.

"Good," he said, a smile coming onto his face as if he hadn't just been in a murderous rage moments before. "I'm excited for our wedding night. And all of the nights following it."

"Me too," I stammered.

He put his arm around me and pulled me back toward the tavern. Moments later, I was back where I had been, sitting on his lap surrounded by Xander's group of advisors, which my dad and Geoffrey were now officially a part of. I laughed when I was supposed to laugh and kept quiet despite some of the truly horrendous opinions the council had about females in the pack.

They got more and more drunk as time went on, and at some point, I'd overstayed my welcome.

"Go, Gisela," Xander said, pushing me off his lap.

He didn't have to tell me twice.

The party was even more raucous than it was before, but I spotted Hailey talking to one of our few friends in our pack. I locked eyes with her, and she immediately understood, mouthing *bathroom* to me.

We got there at the same time, bursting through the doors.

"Everyone out," Hailey said to the two shifters messing around with their makeup at the sink.

"What's your problem?" one of the females asked.

"Just go," Hailey growled in the way that only she could pull off. "Or, do you really want to piss off our Alpha's future wife?"

The others rolled their eyes and did as she said.

"We need to go through with the plan," I mumbled once they were gone and down the hall. "I can't do this. We have to go right now, while Xander is drunk off his ass. As fast as possible."

"Okay." Hailey paused, thinking things through for a moment. "We'll go to your house first and grab some stuff, then my place, then we'll hit the road."

"You're sure you want to leave?" I asked.

"Hell yeah. I hate this place, and there's nothing here for me in this pack, anyway." She snorted. "Plus, starting over in a place where women aren't treated like shit sounds like a good plan to me. Let's go."

We slipped out of the bathroom, then out the back door. The town was small, and my house wasn't far by foot. We ran, taking side streets and hoping that everyone was still celebrating the wedding that wasn't going to happen.

I let myself in the back door and went to my room, stuffing clothes, underwear, and some toiletries into a worn duffel bag. Once I was done, I went straight to the back door again, not bothering to look around one last time. I wasn't going to miss a single thing about this house or my family. I'd been a pawn for them ever since I was born, and they realized that I was beautiful enough to be given to a man. That was all I was to them.

Next, we ran to Hailey's apartment, playing it cool around the few people lingering nearby. She took even less time than I did to get her things together, and we hopped in her car. Neither of us spoke until we were outside of the town limits.

"Okay," I said, letting out a shaky breath. "Now what?"

"Now we drive," Hailey said.

"Where?"

"As far from this hellhole as possible." She shrugged, gunning it onto the highway. "Let's head west. Out of the region."

I ran my thumb over my phone case.

"They're going to be shocked that I'm gone. I should have left a note or something. Nothing sentimental, of course, but more of a 'screw you' thing. I guess I could text."

"Agreed. Let's wait until we're at a new town where we can pick up a burner phone," Hailey said. "They might be able to track us if we keep the ones we have. We probably should have ditched them before we left, but, you know, time was of the essence and all that."

I nodded, sinking down in the cloth seat and watching the trees zip by. Eventually, we drove out of Alabama and crossed into Mississippi. It didn't feel real. It was almost too easy. Then again, we hadn't even been gone an hour yet. What if they were already hunting us down? Gods, what would they do to us if we were found?

I didn't want to think about that. Instead, I stayed quiet. Hailey sensed that I wasn't in the mood to chat—it was already three in the morning—and didn't say anything until we reached a gas station run by a wolf shifter a few miles away. I didn't want to stop, but we were low on gas. Besides, if we waited to get rid of our phones and get cash closer to our destination, there was a chance they could track us down more easily.

Both of us took turns clearing our bank accounts, and we each bought a burner phone. Before I activated mine, I opened my text app on my old phone to tell my family that I was gone for good and that I was breaking off my engagement.

How could I distill twenty-eight years of misery into a single text? I blinked back tears, my thumbs hovering over my phone's screen. It was impossible to explain how much they'd beat me down over the years. All the times I was told to shut up, to be subservient, to be what they needed me to be. All the times they broke my trust and boundaries.

So I went with a simple message: *I can't marry Xander, so I'm ending our engagement and my connection with our pack. I left, and I am not coming back. Don't look for me. I don't want to be found.*

"Okay," I said, turning off my old phone after the message was delivered and crushing it in my fist. Hailey grinned, doing the same to her phone. "Let's keep going west."

2

DEX

Thank the gods that magic beings didn't spread photos of themselves or others across the internet the way humans did. I'd never get away with a relatively anonymous night out otherwise. Here, hundreds of miles away from my headquarters and an hour away from any pack's headquarters, I could be a regular dragon shifter instead of Dex, dragon shifter Ruler.

I finished off my bottle of shifter mead and scanned the room. It was fascinating to watch people when no one knew who I was. Normally, whenever I was in a room, everyone either jumped at the opportunity to serve me or didn't meet my eye out of respect. That got in the way of finding a beautiful woman to spend one night with.

Well, that and the fact that being Ruler drew all the wrong women to me—ones that were after all the power and wealth that being like a king brought. How did High Rulers know which people were talking to them for the right reasons? They were even more powerful than I was, ruling over all of the beings in a region, so they probably had it even worse.

"You on the prowl, Dex? Maybe for a nice dragon shifter to settle down with?" my best friend Simeon asked, a teasing lilt in his voice.

I snorted. He used to be in my shoes—as the wolf shifter Ruler of our region, women threw themselves at him for a piece of power. But then he'd found his mate, Elyse. He'd been almost insufferable ever since with how much he gushed about her and relationships in general. But a mate bond was far more intense than even the deepest romantic relationships, so I didn't blame him for talking about it.

A bartender appeared with a fresh round of drinks, as if he were watching us to see when we finished. He bowed his head in deference and stepped away. I glanced around to see if anyone noticed how he treated us, and luckily, no one did. Without our security right around us, most only sensed our power and steered clear, not connecting the dots between that and who we were.

"Of course not," I said, taking my drink. "You know I've learned my lesson."

Simeon let out a quiet grunt of acknowledgment but left it at that. Yes, it had been fifty years since I'd had my heart torn out and torched by a woman who I thought loved me for who I was instead of for my status, but decades didn't feel like much when you were essentially immortal. My wounds were still so raw that I didn't even like thinking her name.

How had I been so naive at two hundred and fifty years old? Her "I love you's" always came before her requests for new dresses or jewelry. She showed her things off to her friends, rubbing the fact that she was the Ruler's girlfriend in their faces. I kicked myself for it, especially when I had to go out like this. I should have remained anonymous the moment I became Ruler.

Rightfully sensing that I didn't want to talk about my past with women anymore, even jokingly, Simeon talked about what was going on with wolf shifters in our region. They were doing well.

But wolf shifters were different; rivalries existed between packs, though not as much fighting about specific parts of land like dragon shifters did. Something in our dragon nature made us much more territorial than other shifters. We liked our space and didn't want to share it or any of the resources with anyone else, even if they were just dragon shifters in another pack.

Halfway through our latest round of drinks, an inexplicable

feeling made me turn toward the door right as it opened. Like someone had silently called my name.

It was raining out, so the two women who appeared in the doorway shielded their faces from the worst of it. But when the shorter of the two women looked up, my heart stuttered in my chest.

She was gorgeous. No, that didn't encompass everything she was. Her features were delicate and lovely, as was her thick brown hair spilling over her shoulders, damp from the rain. I sensed she was a dragon shifter, but she was petite for one. I didn't mind that at all.

I downed my drink in several gulps. "I'm getting another one."

"Already? Or did you find someone?" Simeon asked, looking in the direction of the two women.

"Found someone."

I slid off my stool and went to the bar, the crowds parting for me without consciously realizing they were doing it. The woman and her friend went up to the bar too, though down several seats, and looked up at the menu on the wall. As Ruler, my hearing was even sharper than most dragon shifters', so I heard her speak through the din of everyone talking and laughing over the loud rock music. Her voice had a musical quality to it, light and soft.

"I'm sorry, sir, did you need something else?" the bartender asked me, ignoring everyone else who had been at the bar before.

"The house mead." I glanced down at where the woman was now standing alone, her friend weaving through the crowd to find a table. "And that woman down there—whatever she orders, put it on my tab."

"Of course, sir."

The bartender turned to get me another bottle of the surprisingly delicious house mead, then slid it across the bar to me, bowing his head ever so slightly. I sat on a stool, listening in on what the woman was saying to the bartender.

"Need help picking something?" he asked her.

"Um, sure. I don't know what's good here, but as long as it isn't too pricey, I'll probably like it." She let out a shy laugh.

"Nothing's too pricey here. I suggest the red wine—made by local witches. Whatever enchantment they used on it makes it go down smooth," the bartender said.

"I'll have two of those, then." The woman dug through her purse.

"Your bill's been taken care of." The bartender nodded in my direction. "By that guy."

Finally, the woman turned and looked at me head on. Her large eyes widened even more, making her golden-brown irises catch the light. I smiled at her, a lazy one that women I slept with couldn't resist, before sliding off the stool and returning to my table. She'd follow. I was confident of it. She radiated shyness, so I doubted she'd march up to my table and say something. Passing the table and eyeing me was more her speed, if I had to guess.

"Is this where I bow out?" Simeon asked, raising an eyebrow. He wasn't upset—me finding someone to spend the night with was always a possibility when we went out anonymously.

"If you don't mind." I eyed her across the room, where she had settled with her friend. The two of them were talking with their faces close together, and I didn't need enhanced hearing to know they were talking about me.

"Okay, then. I'll see you in the morning before I head back home," said Simeon, finishing his drink.

"See you."

With him gone, coming up to me was less of a risk. Still, she did what I expected her to do—she passed by with her drink in hand, her eyes flicking to me as she went to the jukebox. On her way back to the table, she looked at me again.

"Hey," I said when we locked eyes.

"Hi." She stopped dead in her tracks a few feet away. I took a moment to appreciate her curves, which she was doing a bad job of hiding in a plain dark t-shirt under a flannel top and jeans. "Um, thank you for the drink."

"It's no problem." I looked at the seat that Simeon had vacated, then back to her. She obeyed, hopping up onto the high stool. "I'm Ivan, by the way."

It was my go-to fake name in moments like this—not a total lie since it was my middle name.

"I'm Gisela." She extended her hand, and I shook it. Tingles rippled up and down my arm when we clasped hands. Mine swallowed hers.

Her cheeks were flushed red, and she looked everywhere but at my face. Her shyness made her appear more innocent. Maybe she was. She was out of her depth here.

"Have we met before?" she asked. "You feel familiar."

"No, we haven't, I would have remembered you," I said, hoping her line of questioning ended there. Any further prodding, and she might guess who I was. I rested my forearm on the table. "Did you pick a better song on the jukebox?"

"Hm?" Gisela blinked. "Oh, um...no. I just looked through the songs. My taste in music isn't all that great."

"I'm sure it's fine. Better than whatever this is." It was a human rock band from the eighties, one I vaguely recognized.

"Maybe." A long pause stretched between us as she bit her full bottom lip. "Sorry, I'm just...I don't think a man has ever bought me a drink before. I'm not sure what to even say." She bit down on her lower lip. "You probably think that's ridiculous."

I did, actually. In what world were men not fighting each other to get her attention? But from the flush that was rapidly spreading from her face downward, she wasn't referring to her own beauty. She must have been young, then, maybe twenty-eight actual years old. All magical beings stopped physically aging around that age.

"It's not ridiculous. There's a first time for everything," I said.

My words put her at ease, and she smiled, making dimples appear.

"Yeah. I usually don't go out to bars in general." She shrugged. "I'm a bit of a homebody."

"What made you come here tonight?"

Gisela sipped her wine, then tilted her head to the side, making her hair fall over her shoulder in a silky sheet. An odd mix of optimism and curiosity flickered in her eyes before she spoke.

"Wanted to try something new, I guess," she said. "What about you?"

"Just a night out. Needed to decompress."

"Hard week, then?" The sympathy in her eyes far surpassed what it should have, given that we were strangers. People rarely had reason to give me sympathy as Ruler, and to my surprise, I wasn't put off by it. She was genuine.

"You could say that." The less I said about myself and my actual work, the better, so I turned it back to her. "If this is something new, then what's your usual night out like?"

"I usually stay at home," Gisela admitted, swirling her drink in her glass. "Or I hang out with my best friend. She's somewhere around here."

She turned and craned her neck.

"So, what would your ideal night out be, then?" I leaned in, lowering my voice. "If you got to make tonight perfect?"

"I don't know." Her cheeks colored. "Maybe trying something new?"

I glanced over my shoulder. "Have you ever played pool?"

"Nope."

"So, let's do that."

"I'm going to be terrible at this," she said with a laugh. "I've never done this before."

"You'll be just fine. I'll teach you." I took Gisela's hand and led her to the section of the bar with pool tables. None of them were open, but the moment one of them saw me coming, they quickly cleared the table and let us have it.

"Huh, how nice of them," she said. "I guess they were playing for a long time."

I breathed a sigh of relief. "Yeah, maybe."

I gave her a rundown of the rules and showed her how to shoot the ball, first by demonstrating, then by helping her with her form. She shivered when my hand brushed hers, but she didn't pull away.

"Did you choose this over darts so we could touch?" Gisela asked, her voice breathy.

"No, it's just an added benefit."

Her cheeks flushed pink, and she held back a smile.

We played an informal game, not really keeping score or trying to win. It was more about the casual brushes against each other, the glances she shot me through her lashes, and the way her face lit up whenever she made a good shot.

She had no idea how much her warm smile was making my lust for her grow by the minute. The fact that she was dressed in such plain clothing made me all the more curious as to what was underneath. The parts of her skin that I did touch—her wrists, her hands—were so soft that the rest of her was probably the same.

"It's stuffy in here," she said, fanning herself after we finished a game. "Too many shifters in one cramped room."

"Want to get some air, then? I know it's raining, but it'll be cooler underneath an awning."

"Sure."

The rain was more of a drizzle, as it often was in Oregon at this time of year. I steered us under an awning to stay out of the worst of it and rested my back against the wall. Gisela did the same, her shoulder touching mine. For a while, the only sound between us was the quiet patter of raindrops on the pavement. But then, she laughed, as if I'd told a joke.

"What is it?" I asked.

"Mm?" She looked over at me, the smile still on her face. "It's just that I'm having a nice time. It's been a while since I've enjoyed myself."

"I am, too," I admitted. When I picked up women in the past, the expectation of sex was laced through all of our interactions. But with Gisela, it was just flirtation and the anticipation of the unknown—I wasn't sure where she wanted the night to end up, and I wanted to find out. Was it that I wanted her so badly? Because for once, I was pursuing someone who wasn't openly angling to go home with me?

"The night still isn't over," I finally said.

"I'm excited to see what's to come, then."

She looked up at me, then flushed. She might have been somewhat inexperienced, but even she noticed the heat in my gaze. A faint hint of her arousal mingled with the damp smell of rain. She played with the ends of her hair, focusing on a point on the ground a few feet away from her. I took her wrist, and she let go of the lock of hair that had been between her fingers, her eyes wide as I pulled her closer to me.

Gisela's breath hitched a second before I pressed my lips to hers. The kiss was electric from the start, taking my full attention and not letting me go. I cradled her head in my hand, savoring the silky softness of her hair. Her small hands tentatively gripped the front of my shirt, like she wasn't sure where to put them, but she needed to touch me right then and there.

I pressed her against the wall of the bar, so my body shielded her from the drizzle blowing into us. Every cell in my body buzzed at our closeness, even through our clothes. I needed them off—a quick round against the wall with our clothes shoved to the side wasn't going to cut it.

"Come home with me," I said, sliding my hands around her tiny waist.

"Tonight?" she asked, the innocence in her tone making me chuckle.

"Yes, tonight."

"I'd love to, but..." She looked down at our feet. "I've never done anything like this before."

"A first time for everything, right?" I pressed a light kiss underneath her right ear. "I'm not far from here, and you can tell your friend where you're going."

"No, I mean I've never done..." She trailed off, meeting my eye again. Her gaze was loaded with meaning. "That."

Oh. I hadn't anticipated taking her virginity. The innocent energy she gave off wasn't an act. Blood rushed down to my cock at the idea of being her first. But her first time was a big deal, and I didn't want to pressure her.

"Then, let's just hang out here." Her scent in the rain was so intoxicating that stepping back ached. Still, I did it. As much as I wanted her, I wasn't going to take a woman home if she was unsure in the slightest.

"No, I really, really want to." She followed me, keeping an inch between us.

"Gisela." I stroked her cheek with my thumb. "Are you absolutely sure? Because I want to make this as good as possible for you, and if you have even an ounce of doubt, I don't want to take you home."

"I'm a hundred percent sure. I know what I want." A glimmer of stubbornness shined in her eyes. "I'm going in with both eyes open."

"If you want to go in with both eyes open, then you know this can only be one night, right? I don't do relationships."

"That's fine with me."

I studied her face to see if she was telling the truth. Her gaze was full of that same steadfast stubbornness.

"Okay," I said. "Let's go."

"Great!" She smiled. "Let me tell Hailey where I'm going."

"Good. I'll be right here. My place is three blocks west of here." I stepped back and watched her go back inside. While she was away, I texted my driver to let him know that we were going to walk home. No need to tip Gisela off that I was a wealthy man. Plus, it was just misting.

When she returned, her cheeks were flushed, but more from arousal than embarrassment. I threaded my fingers in hers and led her to the apartment I kept in this part of town.

Gisela stopped for a moment when we crossed into the threshold. The outside didn't reveal how upscale the inside was, so I didn't blame her for being surprised. My guards, who were always posted near the door, moved to flank me, but I shot them a glance that made them back off.

"This place is really nice," she said.

"Thank you." I pulled her along faster toward the stairs. The building was only three stories high, with two units on each floor aside from the top floor, which only had one. I owned the other units as well, leaving them open for guests or traveling Alphas who passed through. Aside from Simeon, who was staying on the lower floor, no one else was here.

Once we reached the top floor, I tugged Gisela inside and took her mouth again. She let out a quiet groan, surrendering to me. I lifted her, and her legs went around my waist. Her center was warm against me, the scent of her arousal sweet in the air.

I carried her to my bedroom and placed her on the bed. She was stunning, her body positioned just right, and I'd hardly explored her yet.

"Take off your clothes," I said, pulling my shirt over my head and to the side.

She obeyed, her fingers trembling as she peeled off her shirt and jeans. Her bra and panties were plain cotton, but they were sexier than any lingerie I'd seen on a woman in a long time. Her full breasts were my first target.

"You're unbelievable." I crawled over her before kissing down the side of her neck and down to her cleavage.

She gasped as I sucked and nibbled at her exposed flesh, her heart pounding loudly. Her hands smoothed over my shoulders and back as she relaxed into my kisses. I undid the clasp of her bra in a simple motion, pulling it off and giving each of her nipples my attention.

"Ivan," she breathed. "That feels so good."

"It's only going to feel better from here," I said.

I wanted to take it slow since it was her first time, but I was so hungry for her that resisting was damn near impossible. I rested my lips next to her bellybutton, gathering myself, before I slid her panties over her hips. The scent of her arousal, unhindered by anything, was too much for me to handle.

"Gods, Gisela," I groaned before burying my face between her thighs.

Her surprised squeak turned into a heady moan as I tasted her. The longer I explored her with my tongue, the more her thighs fell open, giving me more access. Her fingers slid into my hair as her hips wound, her climax coming fast. After I slid my finger inside of her, she exploded, fluttering around me and crying out.

I sat up and smiled at her limp, sated form. Her chest heaved up and down, her gaze unfocused.

"You okay?" I asked.

She nodded and let out a grunt. The sight of her sprawled out in front of me was too much to bear, so I grasped her hips and pulled her toward me.

"I need to be inside you," I said, kissing down the side of her neck. She locked eyes with me and bit her bottom lip. She didn't have to speak to tell me what was going through her head. "I'll be gentle."

She nodded. I hadn't been exaggerating when I told her I needed to be inside her. Every cell in my body strained to fill her, but I held myself back, easing in inch by inch. I paused when I was fully inside of her, letting her adjust. When she didn't appear to be in any pain, I started moving. Slowly at first, then faster when her breathing picked up.

Our lips crashed together in a passionate kiss as I thrust into her tight heat. Every time I changed the angle of her hips, she gasped and cried out, bringing me closer to my own release. Our bodies twined together as I shifted our position, pulling her so we were both on our sides. I slipped a hand between us and stroked her clit, making her entire body quake.

Her nails scratched down my chest as she came again, squeezing around me so tightly that I lost my breath. She pulled me close to the edge, and I threw myself off with her, coming so hard that my vision grew dark at the edges.

I braced myself so I wouldn't collapse on her and pulled out, gathering her in my arms.

"Wow," she whispered.

The aftermath of my climax was still tingling through my body, so I couldn't speak. She wasn't going to fade into the sea of anonymous women I'd spent the night with. I wasn't going to forget this night for a long time.

3

GISELA

Take a risk, Hailey said last night. *He's hot and interested. It'll be worth it.*

But she neglected to mention the post-risk anxiety. It coursed through my veins and threatened to make me jump out of my skin.

Had I really lost my virginity to a guy I'd just met? An extremely hot guy who was everything I'd ever dreamed of?

The soreness between my thighs told me yes, last night had totally happened. And if the context were different, I would have been overjoyed at how good it was. Ivan had been so gentle, but so commanding, making sure my first time was as pleasurable as possible.

But as mind-blowing as it had been, last night didn't change my reality. Everything was in flux.

I opened my eyes and looked down at Ivan's big, strong arm wrapped around me, savoring his warmth pressed against my back for a moment. I didn't want to get too comfortable and fall back asleep when I needed to contact Hailey to pick me up. We only had our motel room for one night, and we wanted to head to the next biggest shifter town three hours from here to find work and a place to live. We couldn't waste any more time or money.

I paused for a moment, then slid a leg out from under the covers and toward the edge of bed. I inched out of Ivan's grasp, holding my breath and praying he was a heavy sleeper.

"Good morning," he said, pulling me back into his arms.

"Oh!" I grasped the covers to catch my balance. "Good morning."

"Sneaking out?" He kissed the back of my neck, his hands wandering up my front.

"Y-yeah." My body hummed to life as his hand cupped my breast, and his erection pressed against my ass. I wanted to stay so badly, but I couldn't. "I need to get going."

"Okay." He let me go, and I slid out of bed, taking a throw blanket with me to cover myself up. The corner of Ivan's mouth crept up in a smile. "You know I've seen all of you, right? And I liked the view?"

"Oh, right." My whole body flushed as I put the throw blanket down and found my clothes, pointedly looking away from him. If he looked at me with the same heat he'd had in his eyes last night, I would be back in his bed in an instant.

I still snuck glances, though. His dark curly hair was mussed up, and his equally dark eyes were sleepy, even as he watched me. His features were strong and masculine, but seeing him this relaxed made him almost approachable. Almost. He was so handsome. No, handsome didn't even cover everything he was. I was so glad he had chosen me out of all the others at the bar last night.

Gods, how was I going to go back to my life knowing the hottest man alive was no longer in it?

"Gisela," he purred. I turned, holding my clothes to my front. "Do you really need to leave that fast?"

His eyes raked up and down my body in a way that made me want to throw away everything else I needed to do today. Oh, whatever. A little more time with him wasn't going to hurt.

I dropped my clothes again and walked back to the bed. Ivan grabbed my wrist and tugged me forward, making me squeal. His hands went to my breasts and his mouth to my neck.

"You're so damn delicious," he said, sucking the side of my neck. "Every man who missed out on you is an unlucky asshole."

His tone was anything but romantic, but it sent a jolt of white-hot heat between my thighs. My past wasn't littered with males trying to get with me, at least with me as a willing participant. I had been shoved onto so many males by my family, hoping they wanted to marry me, for ages. I had never been so glad that my pack was strict about women and their virginity. Anyone else wouldn't have measured up to Ivan.

He laid me back down on the bed, sliding next to me. My legs parted almost unconsciously, just wide enough for his hand. I was already soaking wet, and he'd hardly touched me.

"So perfectly tight," he said as he slid a finger inside of me, as if he were entering me with his cock again.

I lay back and let him pamper me. I doubted I was going to have sex again any time soon, so why not enjoy this? His mouth went to my breast, and my hand dug into his soft, dark curls. He explored me in a way I had never felt brave enough to do, circling my clit with his thumb and searching for the spots that made me whimper.

"I think I'm going to—" My orgasm cut me off, rocking through my body. Ivan's warm, pleased words streamed in one ear and pinged around my brain.

I sagged against the mattress. I wanted more of that feeling forever. But it was just today, and that was how it needed to be. Or at least, that was what I assumed.

"Tonight... Well, last night... That was it, right?" I asked once I could speak again. "Since neither of us wants a relationship?"

"Yeah," he said. "That was it."

He was so matter of fact about it. I wondered how many women he'd given that same speech to in bed like this, after he made them come with a few skillful strokes of his fingers. The thought made my heart sink, even though I had no claim to him.

"Okay." I sat up. His erection was rock hard, and seeing it in the light was a whole different experience. That had been inside of me?

I wanted to please him, too, just to round out the experience. I was starting a new life. Why not try something completely new? But I didn't know how to approach the topic.

Somehow, he read me astonishingly well, taking my hand in his and guiding it to his cock. It was hot and hard, though his skin was soft. He wrapped his hand around mine and guided them up and down. My eyes traveled from his cock to his heaving chest to his face, contorted with pleasure. I emblazoned the sight of him climaxing into my memory. It was so intimate, yet so erotic.

How many things in life were like this? So new to me but so great? As nervous as I was about finding a new place and a job, at least I had new experiences to look forward to.

Ivan slumped against the pillows, his body relaxed, and reached for a tissue on his nightstand. He cleaned up and tossed the tissue in the trash.

"Feel free to use the shower first if you'd like," he said. "I can hop in later."

A shower sounded like a good idea. I went to the bathroom to clean up. While I was there, I texted Hailey the address and that I was ready to leave. She was only five minutes away. By the time I got out, Ivan was up, looking down at his phone with a slight frown on his face. He had put his boxers back on, not that it made it any easier to see his shirtless, powerful form in broad daylight.

"Thank you?" I said, unable to keep the question out of my voice. What was the protocol for leaving after a one-night stand? "Um, I had a nice time."

"I did too." He stood, crossing toward me and resting a hand on my lower back. "Do you need a ride?"

"No, I have one. My friend is on her way. She'll be here in a minute or two."

"Okay, let me walk you out, then."

The apartment was even fancier in the daytime, light coming in and brightening all the white and light-colored furniture. It was a good reminder that this was the last place I should have been. My upbringing had been modest, and I had no idea what to do with people who ran in circles like this.

The sound of Hailey's old car roaring down the road was the last push I needed to put this night behind me.

"Bye, Gisela," Ivan said, resting his hand on the doorknob.

"Bye, Ivan." I tilted my head back to look him in the eye, and he took that moment to press a kiss to my lips. Then, he opened the door for me.

Before I did or said anything reckless, I stepped outside. Ivan lingered in the doorway, waiting for Hailey to pull up. I gave him one more wave before I got into the car. Hailey was about to explode at the seams with questions, but she stayed silent until we were on the main road.

"Gisela!" she practically screamed. "Tell me everything!"

"Oh, gods," I said with a sigh. "It was amazing."

"Yes!" She sped past a human in a car going ten miles below the speed limit.

"A ten out of ten by far." I sank into the cracked vinyl seat. "It was like he took everything I wanted out of my head and made it happen."

The part of me that grew up in a pack that treated sex like something only for men to enjoy came roaring to life, tinging my excellent night with a film of shame. Was I wrong for enjoying it so much? No, that wasn't the issue. The weight in my stomach sank more and more.

Hailey glanced over at me, then looked back at the road. "Why do you look so upset about it?"

"Because!" I bit my bottom lip, trying to gather my swirling thoughts. "I just ended things with Xander a week ago. Barely."

"And Xander sucks. You ended it for a damn good reason. Do you really think the thought of giving you pleasure would cross his mind? Ever?" She scoffed. "He probably doesn't even know how to give a woman an orgasm."

"I know, but I can't help feeling kind of guilty." I rested my head against the window. "Which is stupid, isn't it?"

"No, you're just a kind person." Hailey switched lanes and gunned it past a semi-truck. "Way kinder than me, anyway."

"But I might have put Ivan at risk," I pointed out. "What if Xander comes and tries to rough him up because we slept together?"

"The chances are pretty small. Busting in at the tavern and making a scene, or having his lackeys do so, seems like more his speed."

Again, Hailey was right. And even though I hadn't seen him shift, Ivan radiated strength and power. If he and Xander got into a fight, I had no doubt that Ivan would win. There was nothing to worry about.

I took a deep breath and let it out. No regrets. Well, one minor regret—I'd never see Ivan again. He hadn't even asked for my number, which was both disappointing and a relief. I didn't want to turn him down, but I didn't want anyone to be able to track me down.

Hailey and I's conversation drifted to what we wanted to do when we reached the dragon shifter town we'd set our eyes on. It was the dragon shifter capital, sort of. The dragon shifter Ruler had his headquarters there, and because of that, there were a lot of opportunities and businesses in the area to support him and the important people who visited.

Plus, it was easier to hide in a busy place than some super small town.

We arrived around noon, pulling down the main drag and looking around. It was perfect, bustling with activity and lots of "Now Hiring" signs in windows. My stomach turned. I'd never had a proper job before—just cooking and cleaning for my family or doing some odd jobs around our town. But that was enough, right? I'd clean an entire mansion by hand if it meant getting a job that supported me.

"Do you want to find a place to live first? Or at least a place to stay overnight?" Hailey asked. "Then go on the job hunt? I don't want us to sleep in the car tonight."

"That's a good plan."

We parked in a lot behind a small general store at the end of the main road. The store was bright and approachable, so we went inside. It was surprisingly big, with rows and rows of snacks and home goods. And even better, a big bulletin board with announcements and flyers right inside the door.

"Perfect!" I squeezed Hailey's arm and looked up at the board. "Do you see anything for apartments? I'll look for jobs on here, too."

Hailey scanned the layers of papers pinned up to the board, then nodded. "Here's one. But ouch, that rent."

I looked at the paper and winced. I had some savings that I'd squirreled away in the hopes that I'd get out of my town someday, but the small amount of money wasn't going to get me very far. Hailey had more saved up since she had been a bartender back home, but that hadn't paid well, either.

We skimmed the offerings, my heart sinking as I looked at the ridiculously high rents everywhere we looked. At least things were better on the job openings—there were open interviews for cook, maid, and other support staff roles at the Ruler's headquarters. Finally, I found a rumpled piece of paper in the corner of the board and let out a squeal of excitement before I could stop myself.

"We can definitely do this, especially if we get some of the jobs I found soon," I said, stuffing the slips for open jobs into my pocket before taking down the ad for the apartment. "And it's not far from here."

"Let's call before someone else snatches it up," Hailey said.

She called the number on the paper, and the man on the line told us to come right over. The house was off the main road...then off another main road. Oh, gods.

"This is the house?" I asked, taking the paper from Hailey and reading it again. "A private bungalow, perfect for two?"

"I mean, the ad's not wrong."

It was private—the other small houses were a quarter mile in either direction, and the grass had grown up so high that it offered a small layer of protection from prying eyes. I didn't know the exact definition of a bungalow, but the house was low to the ground. And it was perfect for two because living there alone was probably a recipe for getting murdered.

A dragon shifter came out, scratching at the back of his head.

Since all magical beings stopped aging around thirty, he didn't look old physically. But, the weariness on his face and the way he carried himself made him appear much, much older.

"You the girls looking to rent this place?" the man asked.

"Yes, hi." I waved. "Is it still available?"

"Yeah, if you're willing to pay the amount on the ad," he said. "Want to take a look inside?"

I looked at Hailey, who shrugged. What choice did we have? Everywhere else was either too expensive or not even in this town.

"Sure," Hailey said.

The man led us toward the house. The front porch creaked under our weight, and paint chips fell to the ground when the man pushed the door open. Inside was better, or at least that was what I was telling myself. The paint looked fresher, and if we opened all the windows, the musty smell would go away. Plus, it was furnished, though minimally.

Hailey shrugged again. What else could we do, anyway? It was getting late, and we still wanted to hunt for jobs.

"We'll take it," I said after conferring with Hailey for a moment.

We paid the man in cash for the first and last month's rent. He was just as relieved as we were, probably because we were the only people insane enough to rent this place. How long had it been empty?

It didn't matter. Once the man was gone and had given us the keys, we brought our things in, made sure the doors were locked, and went into town for open interviews at the Ruler's headquarters.

"What are we supposed to say if they do a background check?" I asked, my stomach churning as I smoothed my hands over my outfit. I'd hastily put on more professional clothes and put my hair into a neater ponytail before we left the bungalow.

"We can be mostly honest? Say we're trying to escape a bad situation?" Hailey asked. "We can make up some specifics if they ask."

"I hope that works." I didn't want them to reach out to our pack and tell them where we were.

Each of us filled out an application. Luckily, we had the option to check a box as to whether we consented to a background check or not, with a spot to explain why we didn't want one if we picked that option. I checked yes, but also wrote in that I was escaping a dangerous situation with my pack, so they wouldn't alert them by mistake.

People were being booted immediately if their background checks didn't go through the Ruler's system, so I held my breath as a stern-looking dragon shifter processed my application. She glanced up at me for a moment, then handed my ID back.

"You passed your background check, and our system didn't alert your pack," she said, her voice softer and gentler than her exterior suggested. "You can move ahead."

I sagged in relief. "Thank you."

I followed the signs to the interview room. The open interviews were split up into categories, like maintenance, which included cleaning and organizing, and food service, which included cooking and waitressing. Everyone was trained in multiple positions so we could fill in for each other as necessary. There wasn't much competition for the food service job, from what I could tell.

The other two food service candidates and I were ushered into the kitchen, where yet another stern dragon shifter, a woman with her hair slicked back into a tight bun, greeted us with a nod. The name tag on her white chef's coat said her name was Anne, not that she told us that herself.

"Don't be fooled—your position may be in food service, but you'll be cooking meals for the Ruler and his advisors," Anne said, pacing back and forth in front of us. "Ruler Dexter has discerning taste, so he expects the best for himself and those closest to him. I can train you all to be good servers easily, but you should already know how to cook. I need each of you to make his favorite dish, pasta. I'll taste each one and determine who will be selected."

My heart pounded. I knew of Ruler Dexter, even though I wasn't from his region, but the extent of my knowledge ended with his name and title. Was he an asshole? The kind who'd send food back for the most minor mistake? I was so out of my depth.

I expected Anne to give us more directions—"pasta" was so vague

—but she didn't. That was probably on purpose, though. She showed us the enormous fridge, the stove, and the pans, then told us to go at it.

The three of us lunged toward the fridge as if we were going to win millions of dollars instead of a minimum wage job. I scanned what was in the fridge and assumed that his favorites were there, so I had a lot of possible dishes to make.

Luckily, I had a lot of great pasta recipes up my sleeve, and I whipped up some fresh pasta with a meat sauce that even my family had complimented me on. But what if he wanted something fancy? I wasn't fancy, although my food tasted good. When Anne tasted it, her eyes lit up in a way I hadn't thought possible. Way more than they had for the other two.

"This is excellent, Gisela," she said.

"Thank you," I replied, my cheeks flushing.

After some quick deliberating with the dragon shifter who had gone over our applications, Anne came back to us with her decision.

"Congratulations, Gisela," she said. "You're our newest employee. In fact, I'd like you to make the same meal and serve it to Ruler Dexter."

"Right now?" I asked, my voice leaping up several octaves. "I'm hired?"

"Yes, obviously. You passed our background check, and you've demonstrated that you have the necessary skills." She nodded to the kitchen. "Get to it, please."

I'd made the pasta hundreds of times, so I let muscle memory take over. Anne watched me at every step, hovering over my shoulder as if she were making sure I wasn't tainting the food somehow.

Once I was finished, she served up a small portion for each of us to taste. After we did, she sprinkled some mysterious drops into the bowl, which tinged the steam coming off the food green for a moment. Was she testing for poison? That made sense. I was serving the Ruler, after all.

"Come with me," Anne said. "This will be your first lesson in service."

She showed me the proper silverware to give him and gathered up the plate.

Then, she led me down a hallway without ceremony. The headquarters had the longest hallways I'd ever been in, going on and on no matter how many times we turned. Right when I worried we'd have to go down yet another hallway, we stopped in front of a large, imposing door. Anne knocked on it three times and stepped back.

"Come in," a deep, male voice said. The sound of it sent a shiver down my spine.

Anne opened the door, revealing a large room, half office, half sitting space with a table, chairs, and ottoman. And sitting at the table was Ivan, looking just as handsome as I had left him. My cheeks flushed. He hadn't mentioned that he worked for Ruler Dexter. It made sense—someone who worked this closely to the Ruler had to make good money.

"Sir, I've brought you dinner," Anne said, her voice soft and deferential. "This is our newest member of our food service staff, Gisela."

He studied me, his eyes much more serious than they had been last night.

The reality of the situation started to click into place. No one else was in the room. I stared down at the ground, my whole body heating up in mortification.

Ivan wasn't Ivan.

Ivan—Dexter—was the Ruler of every dragon in this region. And he had taken my virginity last night.

How could I have missed the connections? He was incredibly wealthy, and everyone seemed to defer to him at the bar, even if they didn't address him as Ruler. And he had all those guards in his extremely luxurious penthouse. Of course he wasn't some random being.

Oh, gods. I had never felt so stupid and naïve in my life.

Anne put his dinner down in front of him, along with silverware and a napkin. I wanted to bolt, but Anne stood there, waiting for him to try it. Emotions swirled through me like a hurricane. What if he hated it? What if he fired me on the spot because we'd slept together?

I held my breath and kept my eyes on the ground.

"This is delicious," he finally said.

I relaxed. But not all the way. I still had a lot of questions, many of which were probably going to go unanswered. Why had he been at that bar in the first place? And why had he chosen me to take home?

"I'm glad you enjoy it, sir." Anne bowed her head. "Please let us know if you need anything further."

She left, and I followed behind her, not looking at Ivan—Dexter—again. Now that we were out of the room, annoyance took over my thoughts. He had lied to me. A big lie. And now we had to pretend that it was all okay, and in order to do that, I needed to avoid him like it was a life-or-death situation. At the place where we both had to work every single day.

I hadn't imagined my new, independent life to start off like this.

4

DEX

"Would you like breakfast, sir?" my assistant, Kai, asked the moment he walked into my office. He blinked, surprised to see me there before him.

"I'll get it myself," I said, looking up from my computer. I'd come to my office around sunrise to prepare for the day ahead, and I needed to take a break.

Kai paused, like he was unsure of what to say to that. "You're absolutely positive?"

"Yes, Kai, I am." I stood up.

I was more than positive. Ever since I learned Gisela was the newest cook a week ago, I'd been getting my own meals, just to steal a glance of her. And the short walk cleared my head, which was the excuse I'd given the first few days I'd done this.

I wasn't sure why Gisela caught my attention so intensely. Obviously, she was beautiful, but something else was under the surface, something I didn't need to go within a mile of. We'd had one night together, and that was the extent of what it should have been.

But that didn't mean I had to stop seeing her and appreciating her beauty. Or trying to, since she was clearly avoiding me. If I saw her down the hallway talking to the friend she had been with at the bar, who was now a maid here, she darted into a hallway to stay out of my sight, even if I wasn't going in her direction. I didn't blame her. I had lied about my real name—for good reason—and she had gotten the shock of her life. It wasn't every day that a woman lost her virginity to the Ruler.

I made my way past Kai and to the main kitchen, where my staff prepared most of my meals. Anne, who had worked for me for about a hundred years, ran the kitchen with an iron fist. I never had a meal that wasn't delicious.

"Good morning, sir," Anne said when I appeared in front of the kitchen's service window. She bowed her head in deference.

"Good morning." I scanned the staff, who had all stopped to also acknowledge me. No Gisela. Or more likely, she was hiding somewhere in the back. "I'll take my usual."

Anne called out my order, and the staff went to work. I watched, though it made most of the staff nervous, and waited for Gisela to emerge. I thought I saw her, just a flash of her thick chestnut hair, but it was someone else. Disappointment grew in the pit of my stomach. Fine. She probably had the afternoon shift. I'd check back later.

My breakfast—scrambled eggs and potatoes—was ready moments later, and I took it back to my office, a debate playing out in my head. Was trying to get a single glimpse of Gisela really a good idea? What else could come of it, besides the mild satisfaction of seeing her?

It wasn't important, at least not now. I sat at the table on the far side of my office. I ate and reviewed the necessary materials for my upcoming meeting, which was about dragon shifter populations and territories, as these meetings often were these days.

Kai cleared my plate and returned with two members of my council of advisors—Ryland and May, a mated pair of dragon shifters. They were the perfect couple to help me with the region and population issues, since they'd had a child twenty years ago and were expecting another already. They had connections to dragon shifter parents that I didn't have and understood how drastically the population had grown, at least relative to other time periods.

We exchanged pleasantries and got to work. The first matter of business was a conflict between a big pack and a much smaller pack next to them, whose territories were in New Mexico. I'd gotten a number of complaints from the smaller pack about the larger one infringing on their territory for gatherings and hunting. The larger pack hadn't said a damn thing, of course. The only way to get them to deal with the problem was to bring them in to talk to me, so I had Kai schedule a meeting.

Next, we went over the latest census data for the dragon shifter pack that had been growing the fastest. They were on the eastern side of my region in Utah, not far from where I'd recently spent the night with Gisela. Their populations had grown by nearly fifty percent in the past hundred years, which was mind-boggling for any magical being; we didn't die off at a regular rate like humans, so they were straining for more resources and space.

The good news was that large and powerful bear and wolf shifter packs surrounded their territory—dragons were strong, but going up against a bear or a wolf shifter pack in a turf war would be too risky.

The bad news was that they were almost desperate enough to take that risk at this point.

I took one more glance at the data before pushing it to Kai, who was taking notes next to me. "Kai, arrange a meeting between me and the Alpha of this large pack as well. Sooner rather than later. And May, what came of your research on childcare and schools?"

May sighed, tucking a lock of blonde hair behind her ear. "Resources are stretched tight. There aren't a lot of teachers for young beings of any type, much less dragon shifters. And it doesn't help that the bigger dragon packs are demanding more schools and daycares right now."

I cupped the back of my neck, massaging the tension from my muscles. I had been Ruler for over a hundred years, and one thing never, ever changed—the bigger the pack, the more noise they made. And now there were so many big packs that the noise was deafening.

"Then we'll have to find something to quell them in the meantime."

"I'm on it," May said, scribbling down notes.

The rest of the day was filled with more of the same—too many dragons all at once. Financially, we had more than enough money to go around, but the money wasn't worth much if we couldn't find teachers or create new territory out of thin air.

We only had so much land allocated to us, and other beings needed land to hunt and exist, too. Contrary to what some of the most vocal dragon shifters thought, barging into a gargoyle or sprite or other smaller creature's territory wasn't going to work, and not many creatures were willing to sell land to us.

I worked until nightfall, talking to other kinds of shifters who I often consulted with, seeing if they could offer insight from their perspective. They were going to talk to their Rulers, so I had more meetings to look forward to. Simeon was passing through town also, staying at my house, so I wanted to ask him about any wolf shifter Alphas who might have land they weren't using.

The dragons under my care were incredibly important to me, so working this late didn't bother me. The fact that there was this pressing issue affecting so many did.

My stomach's growl brought me out of my daze. My office had gotten dark, so I flipped on another lamp on my way to the kitchen. My headquarters quieted down in the evening, though not entirely. A few members of the cleaning staff, including Gisela's friend, were cleaning up. The kitchen was mostly quiet aside from some soft singing and muted thumps.

Instead of peeking through the service window, I went into the kitchen. It was Gisela, headphones in as she kneaded dough on one of the large industrial tables. Even her white chef's coat couldn't hide her petite curves, and the way her hair was pulled back emphasized her loveliness. She didn't notice me, even when I was a few feet away.

"Hello," I said softly. Still, she leapt back, pressing her flour-covered hands to her chest.

"You scared me," she said, yanking out her headphones and putting them into the pocket of her pants.

"I didn't mean to. You were pretty focused."

Her cheeks colored, even as she looked at me. Then she remembered who I was and looked down at the table.

"What are you making?" I asked, stepping closer and tucking my hands into my pockets.

"Cinnamon buns, sir," she said, going back to her work.

"One of my favorites."

Gisela's eyes finally flicked up, then back at the dough in front of her. "They'll turn out well."

"I know they will. Everything you've made has been delicious." Her small hands worked the dough in a much more haphazard way than she had before she noticed me.

"It's been a team effort." She swallowed.

Silence stretched between us. What was going on in her head? Probably confusion. But what we'd had that night had been pure chemistry, and I wanted a piece of that back.

"You don't have to be afraid of me, Gisela," I said, walking to her side of the table.

"I'm not."

I put two fingers under her chin and lifted her face to mine. Still, she kept her eyes cast down.

"Look at me," I commanded. She obeyed instantly. Her pupils were dilated, surrounded by a ring of gold that faded into the rest of her warm brown irises. "You seem afraid. Or at least wary."

"I am wary. I thought you were someone else, and I learned that you're...Ruler Dexter." She didn't move her face from where I'd positioned it.

I suppressed a smile at her using my full name. It sounded odd on her lips, even though only those close to me called me Dex. "You can call me Dex. But you understand why I used a fake name, yes? Just for a night out where I could relax?"

"Of course. You have a stressful job."

"So, no need to be afraid."

She snorted, going back to her kneading. "I don't need to be afraid of my Ruler, who also happens to be my employer now? Oh."

The corner of my mouth quirked up. There was that little spark of sass that I'd seen that night.

"You don't need to be afraid. I think our situation is different."

"So, you wouldn't mind me making casual eye contact with you in front of others?" She rolled the dough out into a flat sheet with a rolling pin. I almost missed the hint of sarcasm in her tone. It made me smile.

"In front of others, yes. But when we're alone, no." Everything inside of me yearned to touch her again, so I tucked a loose piece of hair behind her ear. A flush appeared on her neck, a stark contrast against her white chef's coat.

"I don't think we'll be alone all that often," she said.

That was true. We shouldn't have been alone together now, as good as it felt.

"If we are, then you'll know for the future." My stomach growled, reminding me of the main reason I'd come to the kitchen. "Is there anything I can grab to eat?"

"Sure. What would you like?" She turned to the sink and washed her hands. "If you want something sweet, I made cookies earlier. They've just cooled. But I can whip up anything you'd like."

"Cookies sound good. I'll take them with me."

Gisela nodded and grabbed a small box, filling it with different kinds of cookies. My fingers brushed hers as she handed it over, making her nearly drop it. I caught it, bringing us closer together.

If I moved another inch or two, we'd kiss. But for me, a kiss was going to lead to more, and more was the last thing I needed to give her. Or myself, if I was being honest. She was a cook in my headquarters, and that job didn't pay well. She had every reason to want to be with me for what I had, even if she'd liked me when she had no idea who I was.

I took a step back, despite my body screaming to go toward her.

"Have a good evening, Gisela," I said as I walked out of the kitchen.

I felt off kilter. How did she make me feel this way, like I wasn't in control?

When I got back, Simeon was in my home office, stretched out like it was his home.

"I brought cookies." I put the box down on my desk.

"Nice." Simeon sat up and opened the box. "Where'd you get these?"

"Remember that woman I met recently? The petite one with the long brown hair?" I picked out a double chocolate chip cookie.

"Yeah."

"She made them."

Simeon blinked, holding the cookie. "She works here? What?"

I explained everything and tasted the cookie. The perfect mix of sweetness and a hint of salty hit my tongue.

"Wow, that's a crazy coincidence. She didn't know you were Ruler?"

"No. I don't think she's that good of an actress," I said. Simeon noticed my frown and raised an eyebrow at me. "I'm fully aware that's what I said last time things lasted more than a night with a woman."

"Yeah, it is." He downed a cookie in two bites and grabbed another. "What are you going to do?"

"The smart thing. Not going there, at least in a serious way." The physical part was harder to say no to. I'd scented a hint of Gisela's arousal when we were in the kitchen, and we'd hardly touched.

"Good luck, man." Simeon let out a pleased groan as he polished off another cookie. "Whatever you do, you should have her make more of these cookies."

I snorted and turned the conversation back to the territory problems we were having. But Gisela sat in my subconscious, making me wonder how things were going to go between the two of us.

5

GISELA

My life in my old pack had sucked, but at least I didn't have to worry about falling through the floor on a daily basis. And I didn't have to worry about the bathroom flooding, a weird creaking sound that happened when I turned on my box fan and my bedroom light at the same time, or bugs that were way too big for my comfort sitting around in the kitchen as if they were the ones paying rent.

I took a deep breath and let it out, turning the faucet in the bathroom sink just far enough. If I turned it too hard, water shot out from around the base and soaked my shirt. Then again, I was probably going to get soaked today, anyway. It was pouring rain, and the wind was making the house shake. My hours started early since I was working in the cafeteria today, so it was still dark outside. That only added to the house's whole creepy factor.

I finished brushing my teeth and getting ready for work. Hailey took the bathroom after me, and I went to our kitchen—though calling it that was a stretch—to make coffee. The only upside to this place was that we were saving more money than we'd planned, so I bought nicer, enchanted coffee that gave us more of a boost.

The lights flickered, and the house creaked to the point where something had to have flown off the roof outside. I peered out the window, as if that was going to show me anything. Lightning lit up the sky for brief moments, and I only saw trees.

I jumped at another loud bang toward the back of the house. Had a branch come through the wall? I rushed toward the bathroom and found Hailey in her work clothes, frozen in place. Yep, there was a hole in the wall, though it was much lower than I thought it would be. Water blew inside almost immediately, but Hailey didn't move. I started to get closer, but she held out her hand.

"Gisela...what is *that?*" she asked in a hushed tone.

"What?"

"*That!*" She pointed furiously at a small shadow in the large hole. A shadow that ran toward us.

Both of us screamed and pressed ourselves against the walls of the hallway. The creature scuttled toward the kitchen, so we followed and cornered it. It was a small, dirty possum. Inside our house. Had he burst through the walls somehow, or had the storm opened up a weak spot in the house? Either way, I didn't want him there.

"I'll capture him if you close up the hole with something?" I suggested, keeping an eye on the critter.

"Okay. Let's do it."

Hailey grabbed trash bags and tape from under the sink, which made the possum run away again, this time through my legs. It took us far too long to catch it and patch up the hole, and by then, I was so dirty that I had to take another shower.

We were going to be so, so late. Anne was going to murder me. She had shown me sympathy when I explained why we had escaped and why we needed a very discreet background check that wouldn't alert anyone in our pack. But after that? She'd been a total hard ass. She wasn't going to blink an eye at the fact that I'd had to scoop up a filthy, wet possum from my living room and put him outside in the middle of a storm.

The storm subsided by the time Hailey and I finally got to work. And just as I suspected, Anne was livid. She pointed to the door I'd just come through, and we went into the hall.

"Gisela, why are you late?" Anne asked. "This is unacceptable."

"I'm so sorry. There was an incident." My hands were shaking, but I'd put on leggings after the possum incident and didn't have pockets to put them in. "A possum—"

"I don't want to hear it," Anne snapped. "You're lucky that you're an excellent cook, or you'd be out of here."

"What's going on here?" Dex said from down the hall.

My heart leapt into my throat, as it always did when I saw him. He always dressed more casually than I imagined a Ruler would—button-down shirts with the sleeves rolled up and jeans. That only made him more attractive to me. He could have afforded to wear the most expensive clothes in the world, and yet he still chose to dress like everyone else. If it wasn't for the ridiculous amount of power radiating from him and the way everyone treated him, he would have appeared to be a regular dragon shifter.

All the tension melted out of Anne, and she bowed her head.

"Gisela was late and was trying to give me her excuse," she said.

"Why were you late, Gisela?" Dex asked, a touch of softness in his eyes.

I averted my gaze again since we weren't alone.

"The house I'm renting is pretty old, so with the storm, things blew off and hit the house. Or that's what we think, anyway. A hole opened up in the back, and a possum got inside, so we had to get it out, close up the wall, and get dressed for work again. Then the roads were a mess, too."

Dex blinked. "A hole just opened up in your house, and an animal came in? Is this a common occurrence?"

"No. Well, sort of. It's an old home, and there are a lot of problems."

"Where is it?"

I told him, and he frowned, visibly stiffening. Was it well-known for being bad? I wouldn't have been surprised.

"Why do you live there, Gisela? No one lives there unless they absolutely have to. I've been trying to get it taken care of for years, but I can't bulldoze someone's house and clean up their property by force," he said. He was so upset that heat radiated off of him like a fire. "I thought our wages were fair here."

"They are!" I said, looking at Anne. "More than fair. But Hailey—my best friend, who works as a maid here—and I had to leave our town quickly because things weren't good there, and we needed something we could pay the first month's rent on right away."

Dex's frown deepened even more, and he crossed his arms over his chest. "Anne, were you aware of this?"

"I was aware of her situation, yes. She got a background check like everyone else who works here."

"Tell me the name of your Alpha. I'll call—"

"No!" I blurted before pulling myself together. "No, sir. Sorry for the outburst. It's just an old pack rivalry issue that doesn't affect everyone, not something that a Ruler should be involved in. Plus, it's over now that I'm gone."

He stared at me for a few beats, long enough for me to feel sweat break out under my arms. Did he believe me? It was the same excuse I'd given to Anne and the dragon shifter who had processed my application, and they had bought it. And no one had found me yet, so she hadn't tipped anyone off during my background check.

"If your living conditions are that dangerous, you and Hailey will come live with me," he finally said. "I can't let you stay there."

My mouth opened, but no words came out. Both of us staying with him? I'd passed by his house since it was on the grounds of the headquarters compound, and it was intimidating even at a distance. And besides, having a stranger—though I was a stranger who he'd slept with—offering a place to live wasn't something anyone did for free.

What did he want in return? There had to be a catch.

"I would need to talk to Hailey first," I said. I already knew how she was going to react—a hard yes, immediately. But I couldn't make myself say the same despite hating our house so much.

"Anne, can you bring Hailey to me?" Dex asked.

Even though I was still looking at my feet, his eyes burned into me. Did all Rulers and High Rulers have a gaze so intense that it became a physical force, or was it just Dex? It was like he was stripping me bare right in the hallway.

"Of course, sir."

Anne disappeared around the corner, leaving us alone.

"Be honest, Gisela," Dex said, keeping his voice low enough that it didn't echo down the hall. "Why would you turn down a better place to live?"

"I didn't say I was turning it down," I replied, looking at his face now that Anne was gone.

"But you're hesitating." He stepped closer to me, and I subconsciously took a step back for my own good. Gods, he smelled nice, like ginger and smoke.

"I am. Because the rent will probably be too high, and—"

"You don't have to pay rent."

"Now I want to stay there even less." I let out a humorless laugh. "I can't accept that kind of offer."

Two sets of footsteps came down the adjacent hallway, and I quieted. Hailey must have been close by because she and Anne rounded the corner.

"Excuse us," I said, pulling Hailey aside to talk. It was silly to do so, since Rulers had heightened hearing, but I did anyway. "Listen, Ruler Dexter is offering us a place to—"

"Yes. Absolutely," Hailey said before I finished. I raised an eyebrow. "What? Are you insane? We just had to wrestle a wet possum out of our freaking house this morning! That place could burn to the ground for all I care!"

"But I can't live off someone for free, and he won't take rent." I glanced over her shoulder at him. He was doing a good job pretending he wasn't hearing every word of this.

"Gisela. Be realistic. We're too broke to pay for a new place, and our current place is a mess," Hailey said, her brows furrowing. When I sighed through my nose, she softened. "Listen, I get it. You don't want to owe anyone or feel like you owe anyone. But we can come up with a solution. Offer something in exchange, like extra cleaning or something."

I considered her words. She was right. Letting my pride get in the way of not living in a total trash pit was silly. But the idea of being at Dex's whims was still scary. The idea of living in that house and having more trouble, however, was scarier.

"Okay, fine." I turned back to Dex and Anne, who were talking on the other end of the hall. "Sir? We'd like to accept your offer, but we want to do something as a form of rent. Maybe cooking or cleaning or something?"

"Good." Dex gestured to Anne. "I can have you both part time here at the cafeteria and restaurant within the headquarters, and part time at my house. It's on the compound, maybe a five-minute walk from where you report in for work."

Working for Dex? Part time? In his house? I wasn't sure why the reality of it was hitting me now, but the idea of having access to his home after being so intimate with him was overwhelming. Like we'd become closer by default, even though his presence turned me upside down every time we interacted.

I glanced at Hailey, whose expression was brighter than I'd seen it all day. Turning him down would be stupid. If anything, I could get over it for Hailey's sake.

"That sounds like a fair deal," I said.

6

DEX

The stress of dealing with territorial fights between dragon shifters used to make getting out of bed a struggle. But with Gisela living with me, that wasn't a problem anymore.

I threw my blankets off moments before my alarm went off at five-thirty, then stopped it before it went off. Gisela was always up before me, cooking up a storm for breakfast. I rarely ever had a cook make me breakfast since I usually made myself something to drink and ate something at my headquarters later in the morning, but this was a welcome change.

The scent of warm, cheesy eggs drifted to my nose before I even left my bedroom. I got dressed and went into the kitchen, finding Gisela pouring the eggs into a serving bowl. She had also set the entire table as if I were having a formal meal.

Since she didn't have to be in the kitchen of the restaurant at my headquarters until the staff prepared for lunch, she was in a t-shirt and leggings, her hair pulled into a neat bun. The selfish part of me wished she wore tighter tops, though I appreciated her body nonetheless.

And she seemed to enjoy that appreciation, if the light scent of her arousal floating through the air was any indication.

"You don't have to make it fancy, you know. You can just put it on a plate, and I can eat it here at the island," I said to break the tension.

"Good morning, sir," Gisela said, her heart pounding so hard that I heard it from across the room. "I thought you'd like a more formal setting instead of just a plate."

"I do sometimes, but you shouldn't have to go through all the trouble." I rested my hands on the counter. "Your food is so delicious I'd eat it anywhere."

She suppressed a smile, though that only made her dimples appear. "I'm glad you like it. Let me make you coffee, too."

"Thank you."

Her eyebrows went up a fraction of an inch, as they did every time I thanked her. Why was she so surprised? Most people served their Ruler regardless of whether they were thanked or not, so I didn't have to. But I had spent roughly half my life as Ruler and half my life as a regular dragon shifter—albeit in the upper class, as my uncle was Ruler before me. Being grateful for something small didn't make me weak.

And ruling with fear and force alone didn't endear you to your populace. It was possible to strike a balance between both.

My gaze followed Gisela across the kitchen as she finished. She moved with the precision of someone who cooked a lot and knew what they were doing.

After she and Hailey moved into the house, I asked Anne to give me her file. This was her first job, though she said she had been cooking for her family for most of her life. And her background was still mysterious, despite having more information on why she'd left— she had gotten caught up in a conflict with members of her pack and her family, and it was safer for her to leave. She didn't want to be found, either.

"Your breakfast, sir," she said as she pushed a completed plate toward me. I purposefully brushed my hand against hers, just to see her flush.

"This looks great." I dug in. I'd never had an appetite this early in the morning until she moved in. "So you've never worked in a professional kitchen before?"

"No, sir."

"You can drop the 'sir' when we're alone." I sipped my coffee. "You're very good at this. Anne says you're a model employee, too."

I was so furious that Gisela had been exposed to the house she was living in that I finally did what I should have done years ago—I bought it and had it demolished. I wanted Gisela right here where she was safe.

"You've asked Anne about me?" Gisela finally let her shy smile show.

"I have." I slowed down. I didn't want her to have an excuse to leave or clean up. "Does that surprise you?"

"Well, I'm in your house, and you see me every day." She shrugged, still smiling. "I never thought I was that interesting."

"I beg to differ." I leaned forward a few inches. "I find you interesting."

She shot me an amused look.

I took another bite of my breakfast. "Anyway, you learned to cook for your family? That was what Anne said."

Her shy smile melted away, and she looked at a spot past my head. "Um, yes."

I studied her face for more clues regarding her reaction. Her family was a touchy subject, but I was still curious. They weren't good to her, and neither was the rival who had sent her and Hailey running, that much was clear. She had barely opened up to me—so pressing her further would only make her close up again.

"They're missing out on great food, then."

To my surprise, she laughed to herself, turning and tidying the counters.

"What is it?" I asked.

"Just..." She shook her head, putting something in the sink. "My life is very different here."

"In a good way?"

"Yeah, a good way."

The pride and pleasure that welled up in me took me by surprise. Based on reports—territory issues aside—the dragons in my region were happy. But none of them had ever told me so. Then again, I doubted that hearing what they thought would impact me as much as hearing how Gisela felt.

I sat back in my seat, uneasiness taking over my joy. Why was I being so talkative with her? I needed to remember why we had both agreed to our one night being just that. Pressing any further with a woman, as much as I liked her, was a recipe for getting myself hurt again. Gisela's sweet demeanor could have been a trap, for all I knew. If it was, it was a damn good one.

I finished up my breakfast in silence, and Gisela cleared the plates, busying herself with the dishes.

My uneasiness changed to annoyance when I saw the first thing on my agenda, a meeting. Two Alphas in neighboring territories were clashing, and I was supposed to act as mediator. Better for me to end this problem now before it escalated up to High Ruler Cora.

When I got to my office, Kai had all of the documents I needed ready, which I quickly scanned. Moments later, someone knocked on the door.

"Sir?" Someone from my security poked his head into the room. "Your guests are here."

"Send them in."

The two Alphas came in, and the tension ratcheted up without either of them saying a word. Off to an amazing start. I'd met both of them years ago. Karl was the Alpha of one of the largest packs in my region, and from what I remembered, he was a hothead but cared deeply about his pack. The last time I saw him, he had buzzed dark hair, but now he'd shaved his head bald and had grown a thick, bordering on unruly beard.

Ramsey's pack hadn't had the same boost in population for whatever reason, so it was one of the smallest. It was easier to remember him—he looked the exact same as he had twenty years ago, his blond hair tied in a low ponytail and his clothes of the last era we'd met.

"So good to see you again, sir," Karl said, reaching me first.

"Good to see you too." I shook his hand, then Ramsey's. "Both of you."

They sat across from me, their bodies angled away from each other. Was it intentional? I ignored the silent battle going on between them.

"Tell me what's going on." I already knew, but hearing it from them gave me a better idea of where their heads were. "Ramsey first, since you filed complaints."

"My pack has stayed in their own territory, not bothering anyone else, for centuries," Ramsey said. "We're self-sufficient, and we never hurt anyone."

Karl scoffed but didn't interrupt.

"I believe that we have every right to hold onto the small amount of land we have, but Karl disagrees. Where else are we supposed to go? We can't take over another being's land, and we haven't been able to buy their land, either."

"You could take them over if you weren't weak," Karl said, not bothering to look at Ramsey.

"Listen to me," I said, my tone sharp enough to grab their attention. "We cannot intrude on other beings' territory, period. Doing so could start a war if you chose the wrong creature to mess with. We don't want this to escalate to High Ruler Cora."

"Would it really be a war if we were more powerful than them?" Karl asked. "And let's face it, if there were a fight between dragons and fae, dragons would win every time.

I took a deep breath and let it out of my nose. I'd forgotten how punchable Karl was. "Then tell me what you think and what's going on from your point of view, Karl."

"It's simple. My pack is growing, and we're powerful. Ramsey's pack isn't. We need some of their land for new buildings and homes." Karl crossed his arms over his chest and shrugged. "But Ramsey just won't give it up."

"Because it's ours!"

Gods, it was like dealing with children. "We can negotiate— peacefully—so each of you can get part of what you want."

"I'm not here for negotiations. I'm here for more land," Karl hissed. "And his pack is the easiest target."

"See, this is why I put this meeting off." Ramsey threw a hand in the air. "It would be more productive to argue with a brick wall."

"If you would just roll over and accept it, we wouldn't have to argue."

"Enough." I opened up the folder with territory maps and slapped them onto my desk in front of the two of them. "We can create a temporary zone that'll be shared between the two packs while we negotiate the terms. Trying to get all of this sorted out today doesn't seem possible."

I held back the fact that they were the ones who were making this meeting impossible. I glanced at the boundaries of each pack and drew a temporary middle ground.

The temporary zone I'd drawn sparked over an hour of circular fighting. Neither Alpha wanted to give over much or any land, particularly Karl, who probably would have throttled Ramsey if I wasn't there.

By the end of the meeting, we had a tenuous zone to negotiate again and a list of rules for engagement for the two that I hoped they'd follow. Negotiating any permanent transfer of land between the packs was going to require even more of this shit. Since the two of them were so combative, I had Kai schedule meetings with them individually for a later date to hopefully calm them down. I dreaded them already.

The last time I'd divided up land between dragon packs hadn't felt this difficult. Then again, the problem between the packs had been over viable hunting grounds, not space to live. Somehow, that was easier.

Ramsey thanked me and left, not bothering to address Karl. Karl didn't mind, of course. He thanked me next and started toward the door but stopped. Then, he looked back at me, ice and venom in his eyes.

"I hope you don't regret this diplomatic approach," Karl said. His threat was so thinly veiled that I was taken aback. He was an Alpha, but he had to remember his place.

I growled at him, and he visibly shuddered. "Remember who you're speaking to. And remember that I'm the one who decides how much land you get."

Karl stared at me for another beat, an inscrutable expression on his face. Then, he smiled.

"You're right. I'm sorry. Thank you again for your time, and I look forward to our one-on-one meeting." He nodded at me and left.

Once the door closed, I slumped in my seat. I hated the uneasiness creeping up my spine. Karl wasn't a threat, but whatever chaos he was threatening to stir possibly was.

7

GISELA

Some days were more than enough to push my patience to the limit. Today was one of those days. I wasn't sure what was going on at the headquarters, but there were a lot of people from Dex's council and other neighboring packs in for lunch today.

And gods, they were so damn *picky*. We had a daily menu for guests and employees, and most days, people didn't deviate much from that besides getting a sauce on the side or something like that. But these people took the menu as a vague suggestion and ordered whatever they wanted. Did it matter that grilled chicken with scalloped potatoes wasn't on the menu? Nope. We had to make it since, technically, we could.

At least I wasn't one of the wait staff. They were catching hell, too, zipping back and forth from the service window to the swinging door to the dining room.

"We need another salmon on the fly!" one of the waiters, John, barked at me through the service window. "This one was sent back. Again."

"What was wrong with it?" I asked, holding back a sigh.

"Not cooked enough." John rushed back to the dining floor.

"What? The last one was cooked too much! I know for a fact that it was a perfect medium!" I called after him. Too late. "What am I supposed to do?"

"Make it again," Anne said. Even she sounded weary.

Fine. I was going to make the best damn salmon anyone had ever had.

I took a pre-portioned fillet and got to work, crisping up the skin first and keeping a close eye on how quickly it was cooking. Why didn't I have extra arms and eyes for this? I had other tickets waiting.

I multitasked as much as I could and finished the salmon, plating it up with fresh green beans and salad.

"Salmon's up," I called, going on my tiptoes and putting the salmon in the window.

John swooped back in and took it away, leaving me to get back to all the other meals I had to rush. I glanced at the clock on the wall. The busiest time of the lunch rush wasn't close to over.

Gods.

In some ways, I was happy, though. Having some random, upper class dragon shifter complain about food was much more tolerable than my father throwing a plate against the wall if he was in a bad mood or my brother purposefully making my life harder by changing his mind about what he wanted after I'd already gone to the store.

I focused, falling into a comfortable rhythm of cooking and plating, until I was interrupted by John yelling.

"Sir, I'm sorry, you can't be back here!"

"I don't care!" a man shouted. "Where's the person who cooked this salmon? The one I've had to send back time and time again?"

My throat tightened, and I froze in place. Anne's eyes slid toward me, but to my relief, she didn't make me go up to the service window.

"How can I help you?" Anne asked, her voice firm.

"I need someone who can cook a piece of salmon." The man slammed the plate down so hard that it shattered. "Is it that hard? A child could do it better. Did you cook this?"

"No, but I'm happy to—"

"Show me who cooked it. Now."

For once, Anne was at a loss for words. She looked back at all of us, as if she were buying time to think of a response. But I grew up with men like this, men who assumed that everyone and everything was there for their benefit. This guy wasn't going to take no for an answer, so I decided to give him one.

My hands and legs were weak, but I stepped forward. It was all my fault, and I had to take responsibility for it. Anne's eyes widened, but she didn't stop me.

The dragon shifter was huge, though not as tall or as muscular as Dex. His eyes flashed with anger that made me step back involuntarily. At least he'd thrown the plate down already, so he wouldn't throw it at me.

"It was me, sir," I said, my voice small.

"You." The man's neck got even redder, and a vein bulged in his forehead. "How hard is it to make salmon? Is today your first day here? If it is, it's going to be your last. I can't believe—"

"What's going on in here?" Dex asked. His deep voice was barely above a whisper, but everyone, including the jerk standing in front of me, went still and quiet.

Despite having lived with him for over a week, I was still in awe of how much authority he wielded without lifting a finger or raising his voice.

"I was coming to talk to the cook who messed up my salmon order, sir," the jerk said, bowing his head.

Dex walked toward the man, glancing down at the remains of the salmon dish smashed on the floor, then at me.

"What was wrong with it?" he asked, a dangerous, angry heat in his eyes despite his calm voice.

"It was overcooked, then undercooked. Now there's a little too much sauce on it." The more the jerk spoke, the more his face reddened in embarrassment. It sounded ridiculous now that he was saying it out loud. I bit the inside of my cheek so I wouldn't smirk.

"So, you're telling me you've come in here to berate one of our best cooks—the person I trust to cook my meals at home—because there was a little too much sauce on the plate." Dex was deceptively still, as if he was forcing himself not to express his anger in his body language. His eyes said it all.

The jerk looked down at his feet, more out of shame than decorum, and didn't respond.

"If you're going to yell at another member of my staff like this, you're no longer allowed in my headquarters," Dex said. The chill in his words sent a shiver up my spine. "Gisela is incredibly talented and works hard here. Everyone does. And I won't allow you to throw tantrums like a child who isn't getting his way."

"I'm sorry, sir."

"The best way you can say sorry is to get out. Kai will reach out to reschedule my meeting with you."

"But—"

"*Leave.*" Dex finally raised his voice. Even the noise in the dining room quieted.

The asshole swallowed and left, his shoulders slumped. The entire kitchen was silent for several beats, my fellow cooks looking at each other in disbelief.

Had that really happened? Did Dex really defend me in front of all of these people?

My heart grew three sizes. I had been screamed at by males far worse than that asshole had more times than I could count. Shoved against walls for minor insubordination. Punished for minor mistakes. No man had ever come to my defense in those situations. They'd just watched and continued on like I was worthless.

But Dex wasn't like other males.

"Are you all right, Gisela?" he asked, stepping closer to the service window. He scanned my face as if I had been physically hit.

"I'm okay," I said.

"Good." Dex looked around at everyone else, then back to me. "You can take the rest of the day off if you need to."

"I'm fine." My cheeks colored. I didn't want special treatment in front of everyone else. They were already confused as to why I got to work as his personal chef.

"If you insist."

Dex said goodbye to Anne and to everyone else, then left. His presence lingered, and no one dove back into working until Anne told us to.

The rest of the lunch rush was busy, but there weren't any additional ridiculous orders or complaints. By the time I was done with my shift, I was mentally drained. At least I got to go back to Dex's and unwind before I made him dinner.

I walked to his house and was greeted by the guards who were posted outside of every entrance to the house at all times. They let me in, and I went to shower the smells of the kitchen off my skin and hair.

At first, I had been reluctant to enjoy the luxuries that Dex had in every bathroom (and room in general). It was too much on top of him letting me stay in the most comfortable room I'd ever slept it. But then I had run out of shampoo one day and used the brand that he had provided. Now I couldn't go back.

I tilted my head back and let the strong water pressure rinse the lemongrass scented shampoo out of my hair. My thoughts drifted to today's incident again, a smile spreading across my face.

Dex was so different, even though he shouldn't have been—based on my past experiences, anyway. He had the power to silence a room and bend everyone to his will, but he didn't abuse that power. And even though he didn't have to, he treated everyone who worked for him with respect.

So, so different than the males I'd known. If I hadn't witnessed him sleepily walking into the kitchen in the morning or sneaking some gelato late at night or any of the surprisingly normal things he did, I wouldn't have thought he was real.

Part of me still didn't believe he was. A small knot formed behind my breastbone. I felt safer with Dex than I'd felt with anyone in my entire life. But feeling safe with someone wasn't the same as trusting him completely, especially with my past.

I'd had moments of weakness where I wanted to tell him everything, but thankfully, I got a hold of myself. Those secrets had to stay with me. I still woke up to nightmares about Xander finding us, and as powerful as Dex was, I didn't want to complicate his life when he already had so many responsibilities.

I lingered in the shower since the hot water stayed hot without me using my dragon abilities to reheat it after it came out of the tap. Eventually, I got out, steam rising from my skin, and grabbed one of the enchanted towels that I'd also fallen in love with. It took me ages to dry my long, thick hair with a normal towel, but this towel dried it in less than a minute.

My laundry was neatly folded on my bed, placed there by another maid that Dex had to clean his home. I reached for my sweatpants and hoodie but paused. The clothes were comfortable, yes, but they were sort of frumpy. I sighed and put on leggings and a more fitted hoodie instead. I shouldn't have wanted to look nicer at home for Dex, but I did. I craved his lingering looks and the rush they gave me.

I was playing with fire, but being desired was addictive. And I was creeping closer to the point of no return, the point where the attraction I'd tried to suppress would explode.

I tied my hair back into a braid and went to the kitchen, the tension of the day melted from my muscles and was replaced with anticipation. Cooking for Dex reminded me of why I loved cooking in general—making someone else happy through what I'd created. And he was always appreciative of whatever I made.

After whipping up a snack for myself, I got to work on making an elaborate dinner for Dex. He loved pasta, so I made it often. I hadn't made gnocchi for him before, so I decided to do that.

I turned some music on and got to work, the familiar motions of making dough from scratch lulling me into a sense of calm. The house was completely secure, unlike anywhere else I'd lived, so I was comfortable letting my guard down.

I heard voices toward the front of the house, and I brightened. Dex was home early. I turned my music down and tidied up the bowls and dishes that had piled up next to the sink.

"Hello," Dex said as he entered. He didn't smile often, but the brightness in his eyes was basically the same thing for him.

"Hi." I busied my hands with the dough in front of me. When

would these butterflies stop fluttering in my stomach? I saw him all the time, and my reaction was still the same. "How was your day?"

"Better than usual, aside from that asshole at the cafe." Dex rested his hand on my back as he passed, even though there was ample room for him to get to the fridge without moving me. Tingles ran up and down my back. "Was yours okay after that?"

"It was," I said. "Thank you for standing up for me."

He grabbed something from the fridge and rested his hip on the counter next to me. His body was so close that I felt the heat from it. As dragon shifters, we ran warm and tolerated a lot of heat, but he was warmer than anyone I'd ever met.

"Gisela, why do you sound so surprised that I'd do something like that for you?" he asked. The light from the setting sun caught his dark irises, making them look a lighter shade of brown.

"No one else has," I said, looking down at the counter.

"That's a shame. You're worth defending." He lifted my chin with two fingers. "Do you believe me?"

I swallowed, trying to look away, but he stopped me.

"That's a hard question to answer," I said. "I appreciate it, but why me? Why have you done so much to help me?"

"Isn't it obvious, Gisela?" One corner of his mouth crept up. "A male will do a lot for a beautiful female, especially if she's as kind-hearted as you are."

My whole body warmed so much that smoke drifted from my nose. Dex chuckled, still keeping his fingers under my chin. He leaned forward for a moment, hesitated, then captured my lips in a gentle kiss.

He owned me completely in that moment. I melted against him, my hands going around his neck. It was as if no time had passed since our first night together. My nipples tightened at the memory despite the kiss being quite chaste.

"Nothing's going to burn the house down if we leave the kitchen, right?" Dex asked, his lips barely leaving mine.

I reached over and turned off the burner that was boiling water. "No, now we're good."

He scooped me up and walked me to his bedroom, shutting his door with his hip. I had never been in here, though Hailey had told me about how nice and comfortable it was.

His big bed was against the wall, its simple design making it even more imposing for some reason. Maybe because I was the only focus, not even a pattern on the white duvet to look at. He put me down and stood in front of me, kissing me again. My head was tilted all the way back since I was still so short despite his bed being high.

Finally, he pushed me up the bed and covered his body with mine, kissing down the side of my neck. His big hands slid underneath my hoodie, warming my already heated skin. He pulled it up and over my head, then made quick work of my bra.

His movements had a frenetic energy that he didn't have the night we spent together, and I loved it. Like waiting to get his hands all over me was the hardest thing he'd ever done. His lips dipped down my clavicle, then onto one of my nipples.

I moaned, my hips lifting involuntarily, and dug my fingers into his soft, dark curls. My pleasure spurred him on, making him tease each of my nipples until I was a squirming mess underneath him. I nearly went over the edge when his hand slid underneath my leggings and slid between my lips.

"Dex, please," I gasped as he worked me with his hand below and his mouth on my breasts. What was I even begging for? My brain wasn't clear enough to put a coherent answer together.

His fingers worked their magic with rhythmic circles around my clit. Each movement brought me closer to the precipice.

Hot, pulsating pleasure released from my core and thundered throughout my body. I couldn't think; I couldn't see straight. My fingers clasped tightly into his hair as I rode out the intensity of the orgasm.

"Had enough?" he asked and sat back while pulling his shirt over his head.

"Never enough," I admitted, taking in his shirtless body. He didn't have a single flaw. Not one. Even the dusting of chest hair was perfect.

He undid the buckle of his belt, then took off his jeans. His erection strained against the fabric of his boxers.

"Can I..." I gestured toward his cock. I had used my hand on him our first night together, but I wanted to try using my mouth.

He got what I meant and slid his boxers off, sitting with his back against the sturdy mahogany headboard. My stomach twisted in knots, but the eagerness in his eyes spurred me on, so I crawled between his legs and ran my tongue along the underside.

"Tell me what you like," I murmured.

"Fuck, Gisela, keep doing what you're doing," he said, his fingers sliding into my hair. He didn't shove my head down or make me take more than I could handle. Instead, he guided me with hushed words, building my confidence by the minute. Even though I was the one touching him, I was getting slick between my legs.

"I want to feel you inside of me," I said, still sliding my hand up and down his cock.

"Come here." He pulled me up into his lap, so I was straddling him.

I aligned the tip of his cock to my entrance and slid down onto his shaft inch by inch. The fullness of him inside me ached for a moment, but it went away when I was sitting flush against him.

He gripped my hips and squeezed, pulling me up, then down. I learned fast, sliding up and down and testing how it felt if I rocked my hips forward. All of it lit up every nerve in my body, taking me to new heights of pleasure. When he reached in between us and rubbed my clit with his thumb, I was done for.

The orgasm ripped through me, making me cry out against the side of his neck and shudder so hard that I nearly came off of his cock. He steadied me, thrusting up hard and fast.

"Oh, gods," I moaned, shaking through the longest orgasm of my life.

He came soon after with a quiet gasp, pressing his forehead to my shoulder. Both of us were breathing hard, in sync. He wrapped his arms around me, pulling me close.

This was exactly where I wanted to be—safe in his arms. Here, my past wasn't important. It was just us.

8

DEX

Rolling over and seeing Gisela's sleeping face tore me in two directions—one way filled me with a lightness I hadn't felt in ages. She was so damn beautiful, especially when her face was calm. And her unique charm had me hooked, too.

And most importantly, everything she did was genuine. Or at least it felt that way. Despite her not opening up about her past beyond what she had run away from, she was honest about how she felt at certain moments, and she had become much less shy, especially in bed.

But was I wrong? Was she just really good at hiding her true personality? As much as she had tried to reject my help and the benefits my wealth brought, the part of me deep down, the one that was still broken from the last time I thought a woman loved me for me, was skeptical.

That part kept me safe and had for decades. I had to remember that. The sex with Gisela was great, but this had to end here—in bed. Nothing serious.

She stirred, burrowing under the blankets until they came up under her nose. It was still dark out, as it usually was when both of us awoke, but we hadn't gone to sleep until earlier this morning. She probably wasn't going to wake up on her own if I didn't intervene.

"Gisela." I tucked loose hair behind her ear.

"Mm?" She opened one eye, then the other, her face brightening. "Good morning."

"Good morning." I sat up, making the covers fall around my hips and off her shoulders. Seeing her naked wasn't helping me keep my distance, so I got out of bed. "I have to get going, unfortunately."

"Okay. Let me make you breakfast."

We went to our separate bathrooms and got ready for the day. By the time I was dressed, she was already whipping up breakfast in the kitchen, with Hailey making coffee. They were obviously close, so Hailey had to know about us by now. But she didn't let on.

"Good morning, sir," Hailey said with a smile, bowing her head. "Would you like some coffee?"

"I would."

She made me a cup of coffee and slid it across the counter. Gisela shot her a look, and Hailey gave her one back, the kind of silent exchange that only close friends could pull off.

"Excuse me, I need to get dressed," Hailey said, disappearing down the hallway.

I suppressed a smile. Had Gisela asked her to leave?

"How do you feel today?" I asked.

"A tiny bit sore, but in a good way," she said, looking around as if any of my guards were anywhere near us. They were told to keep everything that happened in my home discreet, so they wouldn't have said anything. "And very hungry."

"You never eat breakfast with me. Why don't you sit with me and eat?"

She shrugged, whisking eggs in a bowl. "I just focus on you in the morning. And what you want."

"Well, I want you to have breakfast with me." I stood up with my coffee, crossing to her side of the kitchen. In a pan, diced potatoes, onions, and bell peppers were crisping up next to her. I hadn't cooked a full meal for myself in ages, but for some reason, I wanted to make her something. Give her something besides my body, though I was happy to give her that.

"Okay, I'll eat with you." She flushed and gave me a shy smile, opening the fridge.

I leaned against the counter, watching her cook, her small hands moving deftly. She soon had two plates of food ready, and we sat down at the table on the far side of the kitchen, drenched in light from the floor to ceiling windows.

I sat perpendicular to her, our knees brushing against each other. The barely suppressed grin on her face was so endearing that I wanted to put her delicious food aside and kiss her...or fuck her.

I stabbed a potato with more force than I should have. That thought was a step too far.

We ate in companionable silence, our knees occasionally brushing against each other as we snuck glances. I finished eating before Gisela, and I watched her finish up her food. I even liked the way she ate—small bites, but she savored each one. How was watching her eat fascinating?

"Do you enjoy your own cooking as much as other people do?" I asked.

"I do." She held her hand up in front of her mouth as she chewed. "Is it that obvious?"

"Kind of." One corner of my mouth crept up in a smile. "It's good, so I don't blame you."

"You flatter me."

"I only speak the truth." My phone buzzed in my pocket, notifying me that I had to leave. "Breakfast was delicious, thank you."

"My pleasure."

I couldn't wait to get home to see her the moment she was out of my sight.

My mood took a weary turn when I left for my headquarters. And now I had my meeting with the Alphas of the fastest growing packs in the region.

I rolled up the sleeves of my shirt and took a breath, looking around my nearly empty conference room. Ryland and May were on either side of me. The rest of my council of advisors was sitting this one out so there wouldn't be too many voices at the table. Kai was across the room next to the door, clutching his tablet. I'd known him long enough to see the anxiety feeding his upright posture.

"Are you ready, sir?" he asked.

"I am. Let her in."

Kai disappeared down the hall and returned with Yasmine, the Alpha, and three members of her council. To my surprise, Yasmine was noticeably pregnant, though I had no idea how far along she was. Dragon pregnancies lasted a full year as opposed to a human's nine months.

"Thank you for having us, sir," Yasmine said, bowing her head in greeting.

"I'm happy we can speak in person. Congratulations on the baby."

"Thank you." She rested a hand on her stomach and smiled. "He's my first. And I'd like to get a lot of these territory issues solved before I give birth."

"Sit, then. Let's get started." I reached for my tablet, which had the agenda Kai had put together. "I trust that you've seen what we've offered to relieve the strain on your resources."

Since they were hurting the most, I offered to send healers and teachers from different areas to the town to briefly take care of the neediest areas before they went back to their territories. The areas that needed the most help had to find a permanent solution, but I hadn't found one yet. The contract workers already had full time positions elsewhere and only stayed in town for about a month at a stretch.

"I have." The brightness in Yasmine's voice cooled. "And it's helpful, but it doesn't get to the bigger problem of space. We've built out our territory so it's basically one big town. Now what, are we supposed to build up? We could, but that would be a massive project. We'd have to demolish buildings and build skyscrapers. Then where would the people who lived there go?"

"That's why I brought you here—to come up with a potential solution. You know your pack better than anyone else."

Yasmine was quiet, her council members taking notes.

"I honestly can't think of a better solution than obtaining more land. My people aren't happy, especially since we had to build on land that we used to hunt on." Yasmine's casual shrug contrasted the steel in her eyes. "I'd like to buy land from the wolf and bear shifters surrounding us."

"I've approached the wolf shifter Ruler and the bear shifter Ruler about this, and they said those Alphas aren't going to sell any of their land," I said. "The bear shifter Ruler suggested splitting it."

She scoffed. "Splitting hunting grounds? Who does he think we are? That's like inviting in competition for prey. Between the two shifters, we'd strip the land."

"I know, but it's a potential solution," May said.

Yasmine studied her as if she hadn't noticed her before, then went back to ignoring her. I squeezed my own knee under the table. I hated it when Alphas treated those I trusted the most like that.

"The best I can do is provide more resources, incentivize people to train in the jobs that we need, and look into areas of land for homes," I said, keeping the irritation out of my voice. "It would be separate from the rest of the pack, but it could clear up some of the housing problem."

Yasmine's jaw tightened. "This isn't sustainable."

"I understand."

She sucked in a breath through her nose and let it out slowly, like she was trying not to scream at me. "Your pack has a lot of space."

"We do. My pack has been the Ruling pack for centuries, and our population is growing as well. We'll need it eventually."

Yasmine seethed but knew better than to lash out at me. Her neck was flushed red, but it receded.

"I just want my child to grow up the way I did," she said softly, looking at May. "Where we had space to fly without bumping into other shifters and had the best of everything. I'm sure you understand, May."

Admittedly, she pulled at my heartstrings with that. Just for a moment. Ryland and May had obviously been touched as well. I couldn't let emotions—mine or my advisors'—get in the way of my decisions.

"I know," I said, cutting in before May responded. "And I'm trying to give you half of that. You'll have more than enough healers while we train some to be permanent replacements. Same with teachers, though it'll take a while. It's just how this has to be. We can't redraw everyone else's territories as we see fit."

Yasmine pursed her lips, tilting her head to the side. "We could redraw other beings' territories, though. If we had to?"

The thought had crossed my mind more than once, but there were hundreds of magical beings. We'd have to gather the Alphas and Rulers of every last one to redraw territories that had been more or less the same for centuries. As big as the population of dragon shifters was, I doubted High Ruler Cora would embark on that project just for our sake. No one had ever made changes on such a large scale before.

"If we had to, but that would take at least a decade. Probably more. It would require us to negotiate the sales of different pieces of land with different packs, which wouldn't be smooth, either," I said instead of shutting her down entirely. "I'm trying to get the problems fixed now."

"I don't know what else we can discuss, then," Yasmine said, gathering her things. "We'll accept your proposal for temporary healers and teachers. I hope you'll reconsider what the bear and wolf shifter Rulers had to say."

She stood up abruptly, or as abruptly as a heavily pregnant woman could. Her advisors got up and followed her as she left, none of them looking back. Once the doors closed, I sagged in my seat.

"Do you think the healers and teachers will calm her down enough not to attack the shifters around her territory?" Ryland asked.

"The Alphas are so angry," May said. "It has to work."

"It will."

I was positive of that, at least temporarily. The anger I'd seen from

Ramsey, Karl, and Yasmine, on the other hand, was a different issue. Anger made people do stupid things, and anger plus pressure from their packs was a dangerous, unknown combination—one that had dire consequences for more than just us.

9

GISELA

Who knew that sleeping cuddled up to a big, strong man was the best way to get a full night's rest?

I sank against Dex's chest, which was pressed against my back. Ever since we had caved to our attraction again several days ago, I slept in his bed after an evening of sex. We didn't talk at length about what we were, and I didn't want to, at least not yet. For now, I just enjoyed it for what it was—some great physical chemistry, cuddling, and soaking in Dex's calm, confident presence.

I yawned and buried my face into the pillow, feeling Dex wake up behind me. His erection pressed against my butt, as it always did in the mornings. Some days we fooled around in the morning, but we woke up later than usual today. Last night, he took me on every surface of his master bedroom, pleasuring me for hours on end. That kind of sex could wear out even the most energetic shifters.

"Morning," Dex mumbled in my ear, running his hand up and down my stomach.

"Morning." I rolled over and tucked myself against his chest, a smile spreading across my face.

Neither of us spoke for a few moments, just the way I liked it. It was easier to maintain the illusion that everything was perfect and fine instead of...well, whatever this was. Whatever we were.

My heart knew where I stood. I craved the way his presence made me feel safe and protected, and the way he was more relaxed around me. I wanted to see the way his dark eyes gleamed when he was happy to see me for years to come.

But despite having a complete lack of models for healthy relationships around me growing up, I knew they required trust and openness. That was easier to accept as a concept. My past was a raw wound that I didn't want to reopen. I hated that version of me, the one who had been ground into dust after years of punishment and control. What if he didn't like me after that? What if he thought I was weak?

And most importantly, what if he used my past against me? People acted out of character if their emotions ran high. Knowing my weaknesses gave him the power to destroy me, and if he did that, I wouldn't recover.

I swallowed and inhaled his clean, male scent. All of this worrying was going to make me sick, and I had a long day ahead.

Eventually, we rolled out of bed and got ready for the day. I beat him to the kitchen, so I could have food ready for him when he arrived. He did have impeccable taste, as Anne had said during my interview, but at least he typically ate the same thing every morning. It made my life easier.

Hailey came in before Dex did, still in the big t-shirt and leggings she wore to bed. Her dark curls were up in a messy bun on top of her head.

"Morning," she said, starting the coffee.

"Morning. No work today?" I pushed some diced potatoes around in the pan.

"Nope, just cleaning around here." She stretched. "Have a good night last night?"

I glanced over my shoulder. Dex was still in the shower, so we were okay to talk.

"A really good night." My cheeks flushed. "As usual. Thanks for keeping it secret."

"You know I'll always keep your secrets." Hailey poured us each a cup of coffee. "You're okay, right?"

"What do you mean?" I grabbed a fork to test if the potatoes were done. They were perfect.

"I want to make sure you feel okay. He's your first everything, and he's, you know, him." She brought her mug up to her lips. "He's not just any guy."

The furrow in Hailey's brow and the concern in her eyes touched me at the most vulnerable part of my heart. What would I do without her?

"I know." The food I'd been tasting turned in my stomach. "Neither of us are pushing for anything in particular. You don't have to worry about me."

"Okay." Hailey bumped me with her hip. "I'm going to drink this in bed. Talk to me whenever you need to."

"I will."

She left, and Dex came in minutes later. We had breakfast together, but we walked to headquarters separately. Most of the staff knew that I worked in Dex's home and at the headquarters, but we didn't want anyone to get the wrong idea by being together every morning.

I greeted my coworkers when I entered the kitchen, then got to work. My cooking was good before, but cooking so much all day made me even better. And to add to it, I got paid to do it. I was saving so much by living with Dex that, eventually, Hailey and I would be able to move out into a place that wasn't a dumpster fire.

I'd woken up without Dex next to me for the vast majority of my life, obviously. So why did the idea of waking up alone put my stomach in knots?

"Order up!" I called, sliding a sandwich and freshly made chips onto the service window.

"Thanks, Gisela," John said with a smile.

"No problem!" Only two tickets remained. "Good thing the lunch rush is almost over, huh?"

"Yeah." He chuckled, looking over his shoulder, then back at me. The way he shifted from foot to foot made me regret smiling back at him. "Listen, are you busy later?"

"I am," I said, my eyes darting around. Where were the other orders when I needed them? "Busy, I mean."

"Oh." He frowned. "I was wondering if you wanted to get a drink."

"I can't. Sorry." My phone buzzed in my pocket. "Oh, no, I have to take this."

I slipped away before he could stop me. Hailey and Dex were the only people who texted me, and I doubted that either of them had an emergency.

But it wasn't Dex or Hailey. It was a text from an unknown number. My heart thumped so hard that it threatened to leap out of my chest. Had my old pack found me? How? This number wasn't connected to my old number at all.

I tapped the notification with a shaking finger.

The text message didn't indicate who it was. *How are you?*

Innocuous enough, but my hands still shook. A wrong number. It had to be. Why would Xander or one of his lackeys ask me how I was?

I let out a shaky breath and tucked my phone back into my pants pocket. It was fine. False alarm.

"Gisela?" Anne peered around the corner. "Would you mind taking over for someone in the prep kitchen?"

"Of course." The prep kitchen was next to one of the main event halls and had much more space to cater events and parties. Tomorrow was a full moon holiday, and Dex was throwing a party for his pack.

I took the long route to the prep kitchen to calm myself down more, weaving between different buildings and fields. The weather in Oregon was so much less muggy than it was in Alabama, and I didn't appreciate it enough.

A deep growl stopped me in my tracks. Someone had shifted and wasn't happy.

"Shift back and stay on the ground or I'll strip you of your Alpha rank." It was Dex, his voice so vicious that I almost didn't recognize him.

An Alpha was growling at Dex? What was going on? An Alpha never should have disrespected a Ruler like that. It must have been serious.

I gripped the collar of my chef's coat, unsure of what to do. My feet were frozen in place.

Another growl ripped through the air and stopped.

"Fine," the Alpha said. "We're not alone, by the way. I can scent her."

My eyes widened. I was downwind.

"Gisela?" Dex called.

I stepped out of my hiding spot and into the space between the main building of the headquarters and side building used for administrative purposes.

The Alpha was still in a defensive pose, as if he were ready to shift back at any moment. His bald head and thick beard emphasized his strong, masculine features, making him even more intimidating. But Dex's attention was only on me, like the Alpha wasn't there.

"What are you doing here?" Dex asked, resting a hand on my shoulder.

"I-I was just walking to the prep kitchen. I needed some air, so I took the long route," I said. "I wasn't spying, I swear."

Dex eyed the Alpha, who hadn't moved.

"Keep going." Dex turned me and gently pushed me toward the door. "And don't say a word about this."

I did what he said. The tension was so thick that it smothered me, and I wanted to get out of it as soon as possible.

What *was* that? My stomach churned, and by the time I got to the prep kitchen, I was so disoriented that I hardly knew what to do.

One of the other cooks told me that we were chopping vegetables, something I could do in my sleep in any other circumstance. But today, I almost chopped off a finger three times, and my onions were all different sizes.

But I managed to last until the end of my shift without seriously injuring myself or bleeding all over the place. At least Hailey was home. I needed to talk to her.

I pulled out my phone to let her know I was on my way, but another text caught my eye from the same number as earlier.

I know you're there.

My stomach lurched, and my knees went so weak that I had to rest my hand on the lamp pole. Who was this? I lifted my thumbs to text this person back but paused. Was that a good idea? If it was someone from back home, texting back would tip them off. I had to wait until I calmed down.

Once I got my strength back, I rushed to the house. I found Hailey stretched out on the couch, watching TV.

"Hailey, I got some weird texts," I blurted.

"Weird in what way?" Hailey's eyes widened and searched my face. "Are you okay?"

I shook my head, tears coming to my eyes.

"I don't know. Here, look." I handed her my phone with the messages. "What should I say? Should I say anything?"

"This could totally be a wrong number," Hailey said. Her voice was almost always reassuring, but this time, her tone didn't soothe me.

"But what if it's Xander or someone else? We could have been trailed. They could have found out from someone around here." I paced, unbuttoning my chef's coat and letting it hang open. My t-shirt underneath was damp with sweat.

"But it seems like they're being nice? Kind of?"

"Xander likes to play games, like a beast toying with his prey." I threw my chef's coat onto the couch. "I don't know what to do."

"Okay, short term solution to calm you down, you get comfortable and grab some ice cream. Then we watch a movie together." Hailey got up. "Then we figure out if these are worth panicking over."

I changed out of my work clothes, taking a blazing hot shower that I hardly enjoyed. When I got back out, Hailey was waiting on the couch with me with a pint of ice cream.

We split the ice cream and started a movie, though the phone in my pocket weighed me down. I couldn't focus on the screen, so I pulled out the phone again.

"We have to respond. I have to say something and see if it's them or I'm going to lose my mind," I said.

"Okay, don't send anything yet." Hailey turned off the TV and scooted closer to me. "Maybe we could play dumb and pretend it's not you, especially since they didn't say your name."

That sounded like the best plan yet, but I hesitated.

"What if responding tips them off as to where we are? I don't know how any of this technology works."

"I don't think that's how that works. Just ask who it is and say you think they have the wrong number," Hailey said, taking the phone from my hand. "I'll do it."

I let her draft the text. She showed it to me before she hit send. Moments later, the response came: *You know who it is. Don't play stupid.*

My throat constricted while my lungs begged for air. Hailey rubbed my back. "Maybe I should just go back home. This has to be them."

"We can't. That's ridiculously rash. Yes, this is sketchy, but it's hardly proof that Xander's found us."

"I know, but—"

The front door opened, and Dex came inside, splitting my focus. Was he okay after whatever happened with that Alpha? He had told me not to tell anyone, but sitting here with Hailey as upset as I was probably didn't look good. I held up a finger to Hailey and slipped out of the room, taking the long route.

I found him in the kitchen, opening the freezer and pulling out some enchanted liquor. His presence was a balm on my anxiety, and he hadn't even turned around yet. He frowned when he looked at me.

"Are you all right, Gisela?" he asked, reaching for a glass. "After today."

I opened my mouth to say yes, since I was used to saying yes. I was used to being fine for the sake of others. But Dex saw through me, at least through the top layers I used to hide behind.

"Just shaken," I said. It wasn't a lie—I was shaken, but not for the reasons he probably thought. Though an Alpha confronting him the way that bearded man had had been unnerving, too.

"Do you want a drink?" He looked at me over his shoulder.

"No, thanks."

"You're sure?" He furrowed his brows, taking me in. "Come here, Gisela."

I obeyed, and he put his arm around me. The fresh laundry scent of his shirt over the ginger and smoke smell of his skin made my heart slow down.

"Listen," Dex said. "It'll be okay. I have everything under control. You're safer here than you are anywhere else."

The deep rumble of his voice brought my heart rate down further. I believed him. He was the strongest dragon shifter in the region, and one of the most powerful in the world.

I wasn't going to run back home at the first sign of trouble. He would protect me every time.

10

DEX

I liked control, and I never had to fight for it. It came with being a Ruler.

But these Alphas were testing me. My individual meeting with Karl had nearly ended up with him shifting into his dragon form and trying to fly off. The entire meeting was him trying to convince me to eradicate Ramsey's pack, and I'd reached the end of my rope. Him growling at me was the last straw, so I punished him by ruling more in favor of Ramsey's pack, making the temporary zone between their packs more favorable to them. It was worse than any other physical punishment I could bring down on him.

My stomach twisted in knots again at the memory of Gisela coming across us. She was so pale, almost shaking, and she looked even worse when I got home. The tension between dragon packs was impossible to ignore these days, and it must have been getting to her.

I went into my office at my headquarters and found Ryland, May, and Kai standing around my desk, looking at documents on the computer.

"What's happening?" I asked. "Why didn't anyone call me?"

"It just happened moments ago," Ryland said, resting his hand on

May's back. "There's a big fire in a neighborhood of human vacation homes, and dragons from two different packs are responsible."

"Which packs?"

My mind went to Karl first. Any issue dealing with humans was a stressful pain in the ass. Most animal shifters could stumble on humans and get away with it since usually, they were just bigger versions of the non-shifter animals. But dragons? We didn't have that luxury if there wasn't a glamour over an area. Karl knew that, and he was the type to make my life harder by creating a problem like that.

And two packs were involved. The combination of two different packs plus serious human interference brought the problem to me instead of the two Alphas.

"Two over in Arizona near the border of Mexico and the U.S.," Kai said. My shoulders relaxed. So, it wasn't Karl. "The Alphas were the ones who contacted us."

"Have them travel by portal, not by flight. It'll be faster from that far south." I sat down at my desk, tension in my jaw. "Have them meet us in the interrogation room."

As I waited for the Alphas, Ryland and May gave me the details of what had happened. Two dragon shifters had been caught coming back from burning down two human vacation homes. Security cameras had captured it all, so we had to get a witch or warlock to wipe that clean, as well as the memories of any human witnesses. The only upside to the situation was that the houses weren't occupied at this time of year. Since the Alphas had contacted us almost immediately after figuring out what happened, we didn't have their motives.

But after looking at the territory map, I had a good idea of what their motive was. They were right up against human territory, the one kind of boundary we couldn't cross no matter what.

Fifteen minutes later, Kai and a few of my guards ushered in the Alphas of the two packs, Ace and Ophelia, plus the arsonists in question, Blossom and Steven, into the interrogation room adjacent to a few holding cells. The Alphas were vibrating with fury, but the two members of their packs had a stubborn set to their jaw that I looked forward to wiping off their faces.

"Sit," Ophelia said to Blossom, almost shoving her down into the chair in front of a small metal table.

Blossom scowled at the wall in front of her. Steven sat next to her, crossing his arms over his chest. Both of them were young enough that they hadn't stopped aging yet, maybe in their early twenties.

"You both have been brought here on charges of arson against human targets," I said, standing on the opposite side of the metal table. "Are these charges accurate?"

"Yes." Blossom looked at her lap, more out of respect for me than shame for her actions. "We did."

"For what reason?" I asked. "And mind you, lying to me will only make your punishment worse."

Steven and Blossom exchanged glances, then Steven spoke.

"We figured that clearing some of that land would allow us to take it over. Both of our packs. It's not much land, but it's enough to build a few apartment buildings on. Maybe better hunting ground." He shrugged. "That's it, really. We're tired of living on top of each other when humans have all this space that they don't use. *Especially* in the desert."

"Most of the desert is terrible hunting ground. You're lucky that you didn't start a fire that spread for miles," I pointed out. "And we can't cross into human territories unless it's an extraordinarily unique circumstance. I can't think of one, but it's something that High Ruler Cora would have to handle."

Blossom jiggled her leg, her scowl deepening. "So we can't have this mostly unused human land, and we can't get any land from other beings in neighboring territories, either? That's bullshit."

"Never address your Ruler like that," Ophelia hissed. I held up a hand, and she backed off.

"What's bullshit is the fact that we're going to use up a lot of time to fix your mistakes," I said. "Each of you will receive ten years in jail with limited time to shift, on top of whatever punishments your Alphas and their council agree to."

Steven's mouth dropped open. Was he sincerely surprised that there were consequences for his actions? If I went soft on him, others would think they could commit crimes as well. Blossom opened her mouth to speak but my deep, low growl made her cower.

"Put them in the holding cells temporarily," I said to the guards, who stood on either side of the door.

Both of them complied, hauling the furious arsonists out of the room. Once they were gone, the Alphas let their facades drop just enough for me to notice.

"I'm sorry, sir," Ace said, looking at Ophelia. "We both are. We've been trying to suppress uprisings like this ourselves—"

"Uprisings?" I stopped absently pacing around. "What do you mean by that?"

"Just local skirmishes with the fae pack to our north, fighting among dragons in our packs," Ophelia said. "I'd say I was happy that they weren't fighting, but they were doing things like this instead."

"Why have I not gotten reports about this?" Maybe it had gotten buried in the mountains of bigger problems on my plate. That wasn't acceptable. The number of problems had been creeping up so slowly that I hadn't realized how much of my region it encompassed.

"We're capable of handling it on our own. Until now, of course." Ace rested his hands on the back of one of the chairs. "But it's escalating. It feels like we're crunched into a tiny space, barely enough room to hunt and live. And our numbers are growing. People are getting antsy."

"You aren't the only ones," I said. "I'm working on the territory issue. And I trust you'll deliver a harsh punishment to those two? We can't be soft on this."

"Of course. We want to deter any additional conflicts," Ace said.

"Good. You're dismissed."

Additional guards came in to guide them out, shutting the door. I dug both hands into my hair and took a deep breath.

"Kai, we need to call all the Alphas in for a meeting and dinner as soon as you can."

Having something more informal attached to the meeting would take the edge off the tension. I hadn't had all the Alphas in one room since I'd become Ruler. That much territorial, dominant energy in one place was bound to spur some conflict at some point.

"All of them? From across the entire region?" He blinked.

"That's exactly what I said. This problem has to be addressed as a whole. Dealing with individual packs is drawing this issue out longer than it should."

"I'm on it, sir. The end of the week is open."

I stood, towering over him as he started scribbling down notes. I trusted Kai's instincts, so his surprise at the Alpha meetings gave me pause for a moment. No, I trusted my own instincts more. This had to happen before things got worse. Conflict was on all sides—dragons against dragons, dragons against other beings, and now dragons against humans.

I went to my office and spent the rest of the day in there, working on gathering as many reports as my advisors had put together.

Gisela's scent, mixed with something sweet, greeted me. I went to the kitchen, where she was singing to herself and stirring something. The sight of her calmed me down almost instantly.

"Hello," she said softly. "How was your day?"

"Fine." She could read me well enough to know that was a lie and not to press me on it. "What are you making?"

"Some brownies. They freeze well." She gave me the sassy smile through her lashes that I yearned to see every day. "Though I don't think many will make it to the freezer. My brownies are amazing, and I'm not even ashamed to brag about it."

I smiled. I was very familiar with her sweet tooth at this point. "Yeah? You're that confident?"

"Of course I am." Gisela let out a playful scoff. "Hailey loves them so much that she begs me to make them."

"I'm looking forward to trying them, then." I squeezed her hips as I passed by her to get to the fridge.

"Speaking of eating, is there anything you'd like for me to cook for the big dinner this weekend?" she asked, scraping the batter from the bowl to a lined pan.

"You don't have to cook for that." I grabbed a bottle of mead and shut the fridge.

"But that's my job." Gisela cocked her head to the side, the slightest pout on her lips. I wanted to kiss it away. "Is it not good enough?"

"It's more than good enough." I cupped the back of her neck. "It's just that I want you to take the night off on the weekend."

She bit her bottom lip. "It wouldn't be a burden on me. It would be fun."

I sighed. As much as I wanted her to take time off, I wanted to make her happy more. "Fine, then. But you'll have staff help you."

Her face brightened. "Deal."

I kissed her, savoring the sweetness of her lips. Which reminded me...

"I have something for you," I said.

"You do?" Her expression brightened even more.

"Yes. Are you hungry? I think it'll go perfectly with the brownies."

"Always, if it's for a treat."

Just the answer I wanted to hear. "Close your eyes."

She did as I said, and I went to the freezer, pulling out several pints of artisanal ice cream that I'd asked Kai to send over from a shop in town. I got six different flavors that I hoped she'd like and lined them up on the counter.

"Okay, open your eyes."

Gisela did, gasping softly when she saw the pints of ice cream. The delight on her face was just the reaction I was hoping for. "No way! I've heard so many good things about this ice cream from people at work! Are they all for me? I mean, I won't be able to finish them all, but..."

"They're all for you."

She looked up at me, warmth in her eyes. "Thank you, Dex. This is really nice."

"I'm glad you like it," I said. "What flavor do you think would be best with the brownies?"

"Ooh, I don't know..." She tapped her finger against her bottom lip. "Let's try them all, honestly. Brownies for dinner."

"Sure, why not?"

The day's problems were far away, at least while Gisela was here, setting up a taste test for all the various brownie and ice cream combinations possible. The pep in her step, her careful consideration of what went with what, and her excitement to share it with me was so addictive. I was fooling myself if I thought I could keep my distance from her. She drew me in like a magnet, and I didn't want to let her go.

11

GISELA

I genuinely wanted to cook for tonight's party for all the Alphas and their advisors—I had cooked for parties for my old pack, and it was one of the few times where I felt appreciated. But I had a bigger, more irrational reason to stay hidden in the kitchen.

What if one of the Alphas recognized me? The part of me that was thinking clearly knew it was a stretch, but the other part of me wasn't convinced.

Xander wouldn't be attending, since Alabama was not part of Dex's region. However, Xander had all kinds of guests coming through our town, and some of them might have been from this territory. And maybe Xander had notified all of his friends that I'd cut and run.

I let out a breath, resting my hands on my hips and trying to get a hold of myself. I had to focus, or I'd mess up the food. We had spent hours in the prep kitchen yesterday and earlier today making a four-course meal. It was a semi-formal event, more of an icebreaker from what I could tell. The Alphas had arrived today, staying in the guest quarters spread across the compound, and they were having a big meeting tomorrow.

"I wonder what this is about," Eileen, another cook, commented.

"What do you mean?" I asked, stirring soup.

"All of these Alphas and their advisors coming. And just them, no one else." She set out bowls for us to fill and garnish. "Isn't it strange? What could they possibly be meeting about?"

"I don't know."

But Dex was stressed out about it, whatever it was. He came to me in the evenings when he got in from his headquarters, kissing me senseless and telling me he was fine when we both knew he wasn't. My throat tightened at the memory of that Alpha moments from shifting, only stopped by Dex's powerful command. And he didn't bat an eye at how shaken I was, assuming I was worried about what I saw.

Something big was happening.

I grabbed a clean spoon and tasted the pumpkin sage soup I had made. Perfect. I ladled a serving into each of the bowls that Eileen had put out, cleaned up soup that had splattered on the sides of the bowl, and added some freshly toasted pumpkin seeds as garnish. Since Dex loved those, I made sure the waiter who was tasked with serving him took a bowl with plenty of them. Waiters swooped in and took everything away.

We got started on the next course, which was mostly prepped— we just had to sear the steaks that we'd cooked using a sous-vide earlier. But that left me with too much time to think. Was Dex in danger? He could fight off anyone, couldn't he? A fight wouldn't break out in the middle of dinner, but I still worried.

I helped to plate up the main course when it was time, meticulously placing each steak after it had rested. I snuck Dex an extra steak since it was his favorite, and the waiter took it away, leaving me with idle hands again. Gods, I was going to go nuts by the end of tonight. I needed a distraction.

"Hey, we need extra hands. Someone broke some wine glasses out there, and they're dealing with that," one of the waiters said. "Can I grab you for a second?"

"Uh, me?" I looked around for anyone else who could take my place. Of course, everyone was busy. My heart raced. What if there were Alphas out there who recognized me and told Xander? This wasn't the kind of distraction I wanted.

"Come on, they're waiting." The waiter looked over his shoulder. "Here, grab a plate and follow my lead."

I didn't have time to hesitate. I did as the waiter said, grabbing a plate of the entree. The dinner was set around an incredibly long table with Dex at the head of it. He noticed me, his eyes following my path even as he spoke to the Alpha next to him.

My cheeks flushed, and I ducked my head. Usually, my hair covered my face, but it was back in a bun for work. The other Alphas continued to chat, not paying much attention to me. I dropped off the plate and rushed to the back again.

"It's intimidating, isn't it?" the waiter said with a chuckle.

"Yeah, totally." I swallowed. "Excuse me."

The air in the kitchen was stifling and humid, so I opened up the door to the alley and propped it open. I stood in the doorway for a moment, letting the cold air hit me.

Then, I threw myself back into cooking. Unfortunately, the actual cooking was nearly done. We'd made the chocolate cake earlier, so we had to plate it up and let the waiters serve it. Most of the work was for them, topping off drinks.

I took a step outside, just to get some air. The party was bigger than I thought, so it spilled onto the lawn now that everyone had eaten. Sounds of people talking and music playing drifted behind the building, where I was.

It was fine. Everything was fine. I had to keep telling myself that.

I wandered down away from most of the outdoor chatter, closer to where the music was playing. The crisp air cooled my skin and calmed my nerves. Leaning against the brick wall of the building was even better.

During a dip in the music, I heard voices in the direction I was heading. My ears strained to hear them, even as I stayed still. Their voices were low, as if they were trying not to be heard.

"I'm telling you, he's going to push some of this diplomacy bull-shit tomorrow," a man said. "We can't accept that."

"So what, are we supposed to…?"

The music swelled again, and I couldn't hear what they were saying. I crept closer. My scent was probably mixed among the scents of food and others; plus, I was upwind. I shouldn't have eavesdropped, but my curiosity was too strong. I wasn't naive enough to think that everything was about me, but I was too paranoid not to worry I had been found.

"Karl, we can't do this," a woman said with a laugh. "Isn't this treason or something?"

"It's not. It's just the natural order of things. The stronger dragons overtake the weaker ones. Then we go for other beings. Humans are a last resort," Karl said. "We're not the only ones who feel this way. We have to work together."

I jumped when someone clanged some pots and pans together back toward the kitchen, laughing loudly. Two cooks stumbled outside with a flaming pan, extinguishing it with their hands. Smoke rose up where they stood. Lurking over in the corner wasn't a good look, especially since people were going to look for where the smoke was coming from, so I walked back toward the kitchen as casually as I could despite the thoughts on my mind.

I'd heard that "natural order of things" stuff all the time back home, especially from Xander. He used it as an excuse to treat everyone like shit—he was Alpha, therefore, he was better than everyone else. But this sounded different, like a concerted effort to take over other creatures' territory. Was that what they were meeting about? Dex wasn't the type to try to do something like that. Was he?

"Hey, there's tons of leftover cake," Eileen said when I stepped back in the kitchen. "You want some? Looks like it's been a rough night."

"Sure." Did I really look that terrible?

Eileen passed me some cake, which I ate standing up over a prep table before helping to clean up, even though Dex hadn't wanted me to do more than cook food. Facing him was too big of a feat right now. Was I wrong about him? Or were people trying to stage an uprising under his nose? I didn't know of anyone named Karl who worked in the headquarters, so that only left Alphas and whatever members of their councils that they had brought. Were Alphas capable of going against their Ruler?

I wasn't sure. But I was going to keep my mouth shut and not bring any more attention to myself. The more I blended, the better.

12

———

DEX

I got home close to four in the morning after dinner, my stomach full but not settled. The dinner appeared to be a good plan, at least so far. The Alphas had a great time, talking and getting along—with the help of some strong fae punch—and they would likely be in a positive mood for the meeting. I needed everything to be on my side, especially since there wasn't a chance of me sleeping tonight.

Rulers were much more resilient than other magical beings, and we didn't get physically tired or need a lot of sleep. But mentally, it was a good reset, especially with Gisela in my arms.

But she wasn't in my bed when I returned. I sighed. She had no reason to be, since she didn't sleep here by default. Just sleeping with her without having sex first was a boundary I hadn't wanted to cross until now. The more thought I gave to her sleeping in my bed just to rest, the more worried I felt. Now was the worst time to fall in love with someone I promised myself I'd never form feelings for. Too much was at stake in my region.

I lay in bed, drifting into a light sleep until the sun came up. The meeting wasn't until later, so I went outside to clear my head. There were woods behind the compound that were perfect for dragons—

tall trees, clearings to dive for prey, and most importantly, a glamour that shielded us even if we soared to the highest heights.

I shifted, stretching my wings in the morning sun, and took off. Being in my dragon form was always freeing, like I was tapping into my true self. The sunlight on my dark scales and the breeze on my face rejuvenated me in ways sleep never could.

Even though there were plenty of prey around to hunt, I was still full from last night's meal. I spotted another dragon, a female Alpha, doing the same thing as I was. I gave her space and flew back to the edge of the woods, shifting back into my human form. By the time I was dressed and at my headquarters, I was ready to tackle all of these Alphas in one room.

The usual conference room I used for meetings with Alphas was too small—they had brought a maximum of two members of their council—so we were set up in the large one I'd used only a handful of times in the past thirty years. When I walked in, the room was full, Alphas sat around the table and along the perimeter of the room. When people realized it was me, they went quiet, bowing their heads in respect.

I sat at the head of the table, where Kai had set up my notes and tablet. A massive screen was behind me, showing a map of the region and the individual areas that packs occupied.

"I'm glad that we've all gathered here on relatively short notice," I said. "I've been dealing with the issues of our growing population and territories with individual Alphas, but I can see the problem has grown to the point where a meeting with all of us would be a more efficient option. We need a solution—our population is growing so rapidly that resources are stretched thin, especially for young families. But my biggest priority is making sure that we go about this diplomatically."

A snort came from somewhere, but I couldn't tell who did it. I gave the room a sharp stare regardless.

"I know territory matters, but peace matters more," I continued. "It's possible to do both."

"I'm sorry to interrupt, sir, but it's difficult to be diplomatic when your pack has very strong ideas as to what they can do to other beings," one Alpha, a man with white-blond hair, said. "They're trying to intimidate other beings—mostly fae and different bird shifters, at least in my area—into backing off, giving us space to use that land. We punish them severely, but the ideas spread like wildfire. We cut off one head, and another replaces it."

A few other Alphas nodded.

"So, a lot of you are dealing with this issue?" I asked.

More Alphas around the room nodded.

Shit.

"They're things that we can deal with at the pack level, like vandalism and things like that," a redheaded Alpha with a thick beard said. "Most of the time."

I was aware of the problems and got reports from time to time, a trickle over weeks and months. But seeing all of them here at once threw the issue into high relief. How had I let this happen? I had zoomed in on the details without looking at the big picture. It was a common mistake when there was so much going on, but I should have been more aware.

Showing my weakness at this point wasn't going to work, though.

"Then send me all the reports of incidents that you can attribute to territory issues. I'll look over them," I said. "We need to take emergency measures, so I'll have a committee look into it further."

The Alpha's council members went to work, pulling up reports and sending them to Kai.

"Let's address the biggest issues first and think of paths forward." I skimmed the agenda that Kai had put together. "Starting with the strain on the education system."

Ryland and May walked through the plans that they had put together, and other Alphas and their councils chimed in. We went down the agenda methodically, coming up with temporary and long-term plans to get this issue under control. Some Alphas participated a lot, while others, like Karl and Yasmine, didn't say much at all until we looked at the map of the region.

Karl and Yasmine *did* have strong opinions on what beings to approach to ask if they had land for sale, and every last one was something smaller and weaker than us. At least they weren't advocating for taking it by force. I had to take minor victories where I could.

We made a significant amount of progress by the time the meeting adjourned, but I was still unsettled. I was a capable Ruler, but these issues weren't going away any time soon. This time was going to test me.

I went home around sunset, my body filled with the same prickling tension as it had been this morning. I wasn't supposed to make mistakes like this or let problems grow. Maybe if I had done things differently, we wouldn't be on the verge of blowing up these smaller problems into one across the region.

I greeted the guards outside of my home and went inside. Most of the lights were off near the front of the house, so Gisela and Hailey were probably in the living room. I was too weary to pretend I didn't want Gisela alone. To see her and feel her presence.

Luckily, she was alone, curled up on the couch reading a book. She looked up at me, her eyes warm, then confused. Did she see my mental exhaustion? Somehow, her seeing it didn't bother me, though the idea of the Alphas seeing any crack in my armor made my stomach turn.

"Hi," she said, closing her book and putting it on the coffee table.

"Hello." I loosened my tie.

"I've never seen you in a suit before." She smiled, looking up at me. "You look very handsome."

"I hate wearing them, but I always wear a suit to big meetings." I took off my jacket and threw it over the back of the couch, then sat down next to her. "Have you been home alone for long?"

"Yeah. Hailey is getting some overtime cleaning up in the guest quarters." Gisela bit her plush button lip. "I hope the meeting went—"

I kissed her before she asked me how things were or how I was doing. I wasn't going to talk about it. All I wanted was to forget myself for a while, to lose myself in her. She crawled into my lap and straddled me with a boldness she hadn't had weeks ago. Our first meeting felt like it'd happened decades ago.

I cupped her ass and tugged her closer, touching every inch of her. How was she so perfect? She broke the kiss and ran her lips down the side of my neck, unbuttoning the top button of my shirt and sliding her small hands along my chest.

"Oh, Dex," she said quietly, resting her head on my shoulder. I breathed in the fruity scent of her hair.

She didn't say more, and she didn't have to. It was as if she understood what I needed without me saying a word. The last woman I'd dated had always done what she thought I wanted to hear—pumping me up or trying to insert herself into the situation to prove she was smart and worthy. But Gisela wasn't her. She was so perfect that a new fear bubbled up.

What if Gisela was just better at reading people, and better at manipulating them? She had to know how I felt for her at this point.

She ran her thumb along my collarbone, then kissed the side of my neck, her lips traveling upward to my mouth. My heart flipped in my chest despite my worries. Maybe she was *almost* too perfect.

But I was too far gone to back out now, and it scared me to death.

13

GISELA

I kissed Dex as if doing so could take away the heavy weight on his shoulders. Soon, the kiss heated up even more, with both of us peeling off each other's clothes and tossing them to the floor as if we couldn't wait to be skin to skin.

Dex picked me up, not breaking our kiss, and led me toward the bedroom. He moaned into my mouth as we crossed the threshold, pressing me up against the closed door and shoving down his boxers. I gasped when he pulled my panties to the side and sank into me to the hilt.

The sex was fast and intense, like he had to work through his tension through me. I wanted to help him, to make him feel better, so I clung to his shoulders and moaned against his neck. My climax rushed toward me unexpectedly when he brought me over to bed and pressed my legs back toward my chest, never breaking his rhythm.

We lost control together, Dex shuddering over me as I trembled beneath him. He braced himself above me with his hand, his chest heaving, and rolled onto his back on the bed. I tucked my body against his, pressing my hand to his chest. His heart was beating fast, but the rhythm of it was soothing in the silence of the room.

"Do you still talk to your family?" he asked after a long pause.

I cuddled up closer to him, even though the question put me slightly on edge. "What makes you ask that?"

"I'm just curious." He tucked my hair behind my ear, then put his arm underneath my shoulders. "I was just thinking of how different you were when we first met again, and your family was a sensitive topic."

I paused, debating how much to tell him. Being in this bed created a bubble of safety, one I finally felt comfortable enough to use.

"They weren't good people. Aren't good people," I said. "It's hard to think about them or my past. It's all dark and unpleasant."

"But you came out on the other side." He stroked my arm. I wondered if he sensed how relieved I was at his reaction—that he wasn't super pissed at me for being cagey about it at first. "And you're a good person."

"You think so?"

"I do." He took a subtle breath and let it out. "I'm falling in love with you, Gisela."

His words filled me with a mix of joy and fear, but mostly the former. A man like Dex? In love with me? I wouldn't have believed it before I came here, but now I was more confident. More self-reliant.

And more importantly, I felt the same way.

"I'm falling in love with you, too," I admitted. "But I don't know what we are."

He pressed a kiss to my forehead. "Let's not label it. For now, can you just *be* with me?"

"Of course I can." I snuggled up against him, my heart full.

AFTER DEX'S meetings with all the Alphas, work slowed down a lot. We hardly had any orders for lunch, and even those were spaced out. It gave us too much time to talk and mess around. Under normal circumstances, I would have been thrilled that I got the chance to make new friends. But something was off in the region, and it was affecting Dex. It took up space in my mind every waking moment.

Seeing him come in, weariness in his dark eyes, hit me hard, like I'd caught some of his emotions. He was the strongest male I knew. Whatever it was must have been serious.

I finished chopping some potatoes for later, putting them in water so they wouldn't brown, then went on to my next task. Eileen, the cook who often had the same shift as I did, was done with her prep, too. Anne wasn't around, so everyone else was slacking off a bit and talking.

"So, what's it like working at Ruler Dexter's house?" Eileen asked, leaning against the large metal prep table I was working on.

My cheeks flushed despite myself, and I busied my hands with organizing some pre-cut vegetables in containers in front of me.

"It's fine. He asks for similar dishes as he does here." I shrugged. "And he likes the food."

"No, I mean, what is his house like? What's he like outside of here? Do you know how mysterious he is to the rest of us?" Eileen rolled her eyes, making my annoyance flare up like fire. She had asked me this before, and I'd given her a similar answer.

Dex was none of her business.

"I'm not that into the mystery," Vanessa, another cook, said. "He's our Ruler, and we shouldn't speculate on his private life."

I liked Vanessa way more than I liked Eileen, and that comment proved why.

"Well, that's cute and all, but I'm still nosy." Eileen snorted, nudging me.

"Vanessa is right. I'm not going to speculate on his private life, either." I tried to even out my breathing. Standing up for myself was still difficult, but I took moments like this to practice whenever I could.

Plus, *I* was his private life. From what I could tell, he worked, sometimes talked with his wolf shifter friend, Ruler Simeon, and spent time with me. He was devoted to his role as Ruler.

"Boo, you're boring." Eileen pushed off the table and walked off.

Once she was firmly in another conversation, Vanessa came over to me.

"Good for you for not gossiping," she said, her voice low. "Eileen spreads it like crazy and makes things up all the time."

"Like what? Does she say anything about me?" I didn't hang out with Eileen outside of work like the others did. "Wait, never mind. That would force you to gossip."

Vanessa smiled. "It's different if it's about you. You deserve to know."

"Oh, no, is it bad?" Memories of being the topic of gossip in town came rushing back. Knowing everyone had formed their own opinion of me without getting to know me hurt.

And gods, what if they thought we were together? I wanted to keep that a secret—at least for now. Everything was still so new.

"No, just curious. She thinks you're getting paid more." Vanessa shrugged and washed her hands. "But that's it."

My shoulders relaxed. "Good."

"Want help with some of this prep?"

"Sure, thank you."

We worked side by side, talking about our days and books we enjoyed. The casual conversation made me feel so normal. I hadn't realized how abnormal I felt back home, like it was me and Hailey against the entire pack. We had a few friends, though we weren't as close to them as we were to each other. But the rest of the pack looked down on us—Hailey because she was an orphan and me because I had caught Xander's attention. Now I had actual friends who saw me for me.

We wrapped up lunch prep, which meant my shift was over. I had gotten paid extra for cooking for the party, so I finally felt comfortable enough to splurge on some new clothes. Hailey was off, too, so after I went home and changed, we went into town.

Since I hadn't gotten any unusual texts lately, going out wasn't as stressful. We hadn't really explored the main road and all the shops that lined it, so we started on one end and wandered.

"Let's stop in here," Hailey said, pulling me into a boutique. "I love the dress the mannequin is wearing. Actually, it would look perfect on you."

She found the dress on the rack and held it up to me. It was cute and a nice shade of reddish pink that looked good against my hair.

"I like it, too, but where would I wear it?" I asked, putting it back.

"You could wear it for your man." Hailey grinned. Dex had become "my man" at some point in the past few weeks, even though we weren't an official couple by any means.

Aside from that time where he'd just held me for a while. That had been unusual, but I'd loved it. He wasn't going to open up and tell me what was wrong, but the way he held onto me said everything.

"He's not *my man*." I picked up a blouse that I saw myself wearing on a regular day off. I wanted to have more outings like this, so I held onto it.

"But you want him to be."

"Yeah. No point in denying that. But he's hesitant." I rubbed the fabric of a t-shirt dress between my fingers. "And I am as well. There's still all that BS from back home—"

"Which he could protect you from."

"And he doesn't know the full truth. He still thinks I ran away because of some rivalry nonsense where I felt unsafe." My throat tightened from the weight of my guilt. "I should tell him."

"You trust him enough to do that?"

"I think so." I rested my hand on a rack. "I feel safe with him."

"When are you going to do it?"

"Gods, I don't know. Soon." I lifted one shoulder in a shrug. "I'm scared he'll be upset that I lied."

"To be fair, he lied about his name. I'm sure he would understand that you lied to stay safe, too."

"I hope so." I held up a strawberry red dress. "This would look amazing on you."

"I love that." She took it from me. "I'll try it on."

Hailey took the dress to the back, and I kept browsing. The lingerie section was tucked to the side. Just the sight of it made me blush. Dex liked my boring cotton underwear, but what if I surprised him?

No, I wasn't ready for that. As confident as I had grown when it came to sex, lingerie felt like something a girlfriend would do for her boyfriend.

I meandered toward the front window again, looking outside. The ice cream shop where Dex had gotten the pints he'd surprised me with was across the street, and I wanted to visit myself.

But happy thoughts of sweet treats evaporated when I saw two familiar men. Both were wearing plain clothing, as if they were trying to blend in. I whipped around and hustled to the back, my chest tight.

"Hailey!" I hissed through the door. "We need to go!"

"What?" She poked her head out from behind the dressing room curtain.

"Geoffrey and his friend Zach. We need to get out of here."

"Woah, hold on. You're sure?" She looked toward the front of the store, and I pushed her back inside.

"I'm sure! I'd know my brother's build and walk anywhere, and Zach's basically his lackey in training. Come on, we need to leave before they find us!" My breath rushed in and out so quickly that I got lightheaded.

Hailey didn't question me—she put on her clothes, leaving the dresses she tried on behind, and we returned to Dex's, taking the opposite direction from where I saw Geoffrey and Zach. My thoughts raced the entire way back. I didn't know whether to run or to stay or if this was even a coincidence.

My entire life here was too good to be true. Me, being happy? Having independence? Having a job and new friends who didn't try to use me to get to a better standing in the pack? Apparently, it wasn't meant to be.

I needed Dex. He'd protect me.

I burst through the doors of the house, past the guards, tears running down my face.

"Dex?" I called out. "Dex?"

I ran through the house, nearly tripping over my own feet in my panic. Finally, I turned the corner to the living room and stopped dead. Geoffrey and Zach were sitting on the couch across from Dex, smug expressions on their faces.

No. This wasn't happening. My entire world shattered when I took in Dex's face. The subtle warmth in his eyes whenever he looked at me was gone, like I was a stranger. What had they told him?

"Come in, Gisela," he said, his voice flat and cold. "We have some things to talk about."

14

DEX

I forced myself to look calm despite my heart splintering in my chest. When these two men showed up on my doorstep, telling me that Gisela wasn't who she said she was, I hadn't wanted to believe it. But seeing Gisela's distress, tears streaming down her face and her entire body trembling, confirmed something was up.

The woman I had started to fall in love with wasn't being honest with me.

"Leave, Hailey," I ordered, my eyes following Gisela as she sat in an armchair adjacent to me.

Hailey didn't protest and left down the hall, shooting Gisela a sympathetic look. What was Hailey's past, then? Were they even best friends? I trusted my people to do a good background check, so I doubted they were criminals. But knowing she had lied to me was a knife to the chest.

"Continue what you were saying before," I said to Geoffrey. He had said that he was Gisela's older brother, and the more I looked at him, the more I saw the resemblance between the two.

"I can explain," Gisela said.

"As we were saying," Geoffrey cut in, glaring at her. "We're from

Gisela's pack back home, and we wanted to tell you that she's engaged to our Alpha. We're here to take her back to him for their wedding."

"She's engaged to her Alpha," I said, my voice flat even as the knife in my heart twisted. The crease in her brow and tears in her eyes didn't deny it.

"He *was* my fiancé. He's not a good man," Gisela whispered. "I never wanted to marry him. My family pushed me into it, and I couldn't say no.'"

"You should be honored to be betrothed to your Alpha," Zach, the other man, barked. "Do you know how many women would kill to be in your position right now?"

Gisela kept crying, but I was simply numb. So her entire story about running away from a rivalry was made up. No wonder she didn't want me to reach out to her Alpha to fix it—he would have told me that she was his fiancé. And like hell was I going to be with a woman who was already promised to someone else.

"Here's a photo from their engagement party, if you want proof," Geoffrey said, pulling out his phone. He handed it to me after pulling up a photo. "Our Alpha is the one in the green shirt."

Gisela was perched on her Alpha's lap. Geoffrey and a man who resembled them both— their father, I assumed—were in the photo, too, further cementing that this was real.

"I dumped him and ran," Gisela mumbled through tears. "I had to send it by text because I was scared of what he'd do if I told him face to face. He hurt me for something so minor at the same party where that picture was taken, and it was the final straw."

"He never received this text you're talking about," Geoffrey said, raising an eyebrow. The flicker of hope I had at her leaving him disappeared. "As far as he's concerned, you're still engaged."

"Did you actually send that text?" I asked. I needed hard proof. I couldn't take her at her word anymore if Geoffrey and Zach had already confirmed some of her lies.

"Yes! Please believe me!" Gisela wiped her eyes with the back of her hand.

"Then let me see it," I said, putting my hand out.

She reached for her phone, then stopped, sniffing. "I sent it from my old phone and destroyed it so I wouldn't be found."

Another jab of pain to my chest. Were lies just falling from her mouth that easily?

"So, you have no proof," Geoffrey said.

Gisela went pale, opening and closing her mouth like she couldn't figure out what to say.

"I know it sounds like a lie, but I did send that text. And honestly, I did lie about where I came from because I was scared. My life back home was awful. I was controlled by my family and never given any freedom like I have here!" She reached for me, but I pulled away. "I didn't intentionally lie to hurt you! I couldn't risk them finding me! Though I guess it's too late for that."

"Doesn't matter. You could be making it up entirely. It's not the first time you've lied," Geoffrey said. "I doubt you mentioned that you've cheated on Xander in the past."

"I haven't! That's a flat out lie, Geoffrey!" Gisela cried.

"Is it?" Zach scoffed.

"Yes! What proof do you have?" Gisela's voice cracked.

"What proof do you have against us?" Zach shot back. "It's two against one, if we only have our word to go off of. Of course you'd deny something like that. You've sunk your claws into him and don't want to let go. He's a Ruler, not just an Alpha. An upgrade."

"You're the liar!" Gisela's voice lacked all conviction, which made my belief in her weaken to the point of almost crumbling.

"Gods." Geoffrey shook his head, his nose wrinkling with disgust. "Our parents are disappointed in you, Gisela. They taught us to be loyal and respectful, but based on the way your scent is mixed with Ruler Dexter's here, you haven't been either of those things."

Gisela didn't respond. She just trembled in place, curling her knees up to her chest so she was in a ball. Like she'd conceded because she had nothing left in her arsenal. No excuses to lob back.

I rested my elbows on my knees, then my forehead in my palm, trying to wrap my head around all of this. Some things started to make sense—her reluctance to talk about her family and her past, for one. If she'd told me about them, she would have had more lies to keep straight. Geoffrey didn't seem like the nicest person, but he also didn't come off as an evil villain like she suggested he was.

I didn't know her Alpha since he was in a different region, so maybe he was an asshole who had hurt her. But maybe he wasn't. She had made up a story about one thing, now everything she said was in question. Maybe she had cheated. And the idea of her skipping from being with an Alpha to being with a Ruler made sense too—climbing the social ladder one man at a time.

The bottom line was that Gisela hadn't been truthful with me. At best, she had sent this text, and he hadn't gotten it, making her Alpha believe she was still his fiancé. At worst, she was cheating on me with someone else and knew exactly what she was doing.

That was more than enough for me to throw away everything that we had together, not that it was real. I thought that being used for my money and status was the worst way a woman could hurt me, but I was wrong. Lies hurt more.

In some ways, Gisela was similar to my ex—she had told me what I wanted to hear in order to keep me. Just because she rejected the benefits of my wealth now didn't mean she'd stay like that forever. Maybe she was playing a long game. Maybe she was as bad as they said. Too much doubt had taken root in my heart for me to ignore it.

"Thank you for telling me," I said to Geoffrey and Zach. "Gisela, I want you to pack up your things. I think you need to go."

I didn't want her to leave, but it was better if she left now, before I got even more attached. I didn't know who was telling the truth, but Gisela had too many inconsistencies in her stories for me to fully trust her. If there wasn't trust, there could never be a relationship.

"But—"

"You're going to pack up your things—and Hailey will, too—and you're going to leave. That's all I'm going to say about this matter." I stood over her until she got up.

"You're not even going to hear my side of the story? You're just going to believe them at face value?" she asked.

If she had looked at me with her big, watery brown eyes earlier this morning, I would have done anything she needed to cheer her up. Now I had no idea who I was looking at. A fraud. Another example of how easily I was fooled by a beautiful woman. A mistake.

"Yes, I am going to believe them. I *do* believe them. They have evidence, and you don't."

Gisela shook her head, fire kindling in her eyes. "So, you're not going to talk to me to get the full picture? You're just going to fixate on what these complete strangers have said and one stupid picture? My life back home was horrific! I was practically—"

"It's not necessarily what they've said. All I know is you've lied to me about something big, and from the evidence I have, you were cheating on someone else with me." I pointed down the hallway. "Leave."

"Dex—"

"Get out of my sight, Gisela." My voice echoed down the hallway, and finally, she turned and left, walking slowly as her body was wracked with sobs.

"We'll be waiting for you, Gisela," Geoffrey called after her, standing up. "You and Hailey can meet us outside. Xander will be excited to see you."

Gisela shot a glare over her shoulder and disappeared around the corner of the hallway.

Geoffrey's and Zach's faces were so smug, like they'd won. They were just the messengers, so I shouldn't have blamed them, but I hated them, too. Why had they come here and shattered the one thing that I could depend on in my life—seeing Gisela's smile every morning?

Then again, better that they told me now than later. It hurt now, but it would have devastated me later.

I summoned one of my guards, and he led Geoffrey and Zach out front. Another lingered behind to escort Gisela and Hailey out when the time came. I walked straight out the back door and ran to the edge of the woods, shifting mid-step and taking off. I needed to be as far away from Gisela and everything that reminded me of her as I could.

15

GISELA

y life was a complete nightmare, and I wanted to wake up. But I couldn't. My throat was raw from sobbing, and my head ached.

Dex hadn't believed me. Two random men with a photo and some made up stories had a more valuable point of view than me, the woman I thought he loved.

He hadn't *wanted* to believe me or hear me out. If he had just listened to everything I needed to get out, he would have understood. What did that say about him, then? That he didn't have feelings for me the way I thought? I wasn't sure if I was more angry or saddened by that. Everything we had was a fantasy.

I should have lowered my expectations. Why did I think I could get away from my old life that easily? It dragged me back no matter what.

"Nothing good happened, did it?" Hailey said as I walked into my bedroom. I hadn't spent the night in it in ages, since usually I was in Dex's bed at night. "I heard the shouting from back here."

I shook my head. "We've been kicked out, and Zach and Geoffrey are expecting to take us back to Alabama."

"Like hell will I do that!" Hailey stood up and paced. "We need to sneak out."

"There's a guard waiting to escort us out. We can't escape."

I sank down on the bed and tried to get a hold of myself, but too many emotions were surging through me. At the center of it all was hopelessness. The future I'd envisioned since we got here was replaced with my old one—being married to Xander and essentially being stripped of any freedom I might have had. Gods, maybe even having his child.

At least he hadn't taken my virginity. But my memories of that night were tainted by the ice in Dex's ink dark eyes.

"No, there's no 'can't' in this situation." Hailey put her hands on her hips and looked at me. "We're going to try something. Can you trust me 100 percent?"

"Of course." She was the only person in this world I trusted.

"Okay, pack up everything. I'll meet you back in this room soon."

She went through the door that connected our rooms and packed. I did the same. I stuffed my clothes into my duffel bag haphazardly and my toiletries, along with some fancy shampoo and conditioner that Dex had provided. Hailey came back in, fully dressed and ready to go.

She poked her head out into the hallway, then came back in, shutting the heavy door.

"Okay, the guard is there. I know him from work, so he might cooperate," she whispered, digging through her purse and coming out with a wad of cash. My eyes widened. "Good thing we didn't buy any clothes, and I've been saving most of my paycheck."

"You want to bribe him to look the other way?"

"Of course! We need to get out of here without being caught, and he's our best bet. Maybe he can help us with a car, too, since they probably know what my car looks like." Her blue-green eyes scanned my face. "What's wrong?"

"I don't know. What are we going to do, keep running forever?" I asked, taking a slow, even breath so I wouldn't start crying again.

"No, but we can definitely run if we have the chance. So this time didn't work, and they somehow found us." She squeezed my shoulder. "But that doesn't mean that we can't figure something else out. Honestly, before we ever left and we were daydreaming about our plan, did you think we'd get jobs and strike out on our own like this? We weren't perfect, and the house we lived in sucked, but we were on our feet."

She had a point. I was so terrified when we left, and up until now, the only fear holding me back was back with our old pack. I did well at my job, had friends, and up until today, love. We could pick up and do it again, figuring out how to escape our pack once and for all as we ran.

"Okay. Then let's do it."

"Yes!" Hailey grinned. "Give me a second."

She slipped into the hallway and ran down it, leaving me paralyzed. What if this didn't work? Then what? I'd happily break through that window, shift, and fly away, then. Hailey gave great pep talks.

A few minutes later, she came back in, a grin on her face. "He's sneaking us out the back door, and we're trading cars with him. He's going to stall them, too. Let's go."

I grabbed my bag and tiptoed into the hallway behind her, my heart pounding. The guard nodded at me and guided us toward the back door. Once we were outside, we booked it toward the parking lot on the far side of the compound, weaving through buildings. I didn't want to look back. I only pushed forward.

Hailey slowed down in the parking lot until we found the black pickup truck. It was plain, but high off the ground, so I had to jump up into it. And luckily, I could slouch down so no one could see me.

"Perfect, there's this hat, too," Hailey said, pulling on a baseball hat that was in the console between the seats.

She turned the car on and whipped out of the parking lot, heading toward the main road. I stayed slouched down in case they had left and were looking for us, even though we'd packed in record time and gotten out fast.

"I think we lost them," Hailey said after we had been on the highway for about thirty minutes. "Or at least I hope so. No one's following us."

"Now what, then?" I sat up in my seat. "Where do you want to go?"

"A city, maybe? We could blend in more with more people. How about Austin?"

"Wow, Austin? Texas?" I looked out the window at the passing trees. "That's really different, and I don't know anything about it."

"Me either. But it's worth a shot. I don't think Zach and Geoffrey would think we'd go back to our old region, even if it's super far away." Hailey shrugged. "Might as well give it a shot."

"Okay. Austin it is."

16

DEX

Every night since I'd kicked Gisela out, I spent the evening in my dragon form, trying to escape my feelings. It didn't clear my head, but it gave me some respite from the worst of my thoughts.

Gisela was gone, period. She had used me, but in a different way than before. My uneasiness about the situation grew the more I thought about it. How could I have missed the signs? Every interaction looked different now. Had she really been engaged to someone else the whole time? What if this text she had sent to break up with her fiancé was real? What kind of life was she living to have allegedly left like that?

But whatever her situation was, she'd lied to me. And I wished she had been honest with me from the beginning. I was more than powerful enough to protect her. Now trusting her would always have an asterisk next to it if we ever saw each other again. That was a big 'if.'

Regardless, I missed her. I missed how things were before, with her singing to herself as she cooked in the kitchen, giving me warm smiles as she told me about what she was doing. The comfort of having her in my arms, and the intoxicating scent of her arousal.

Even if I had been completely ignorant of her lies, I'd been happier.

Today's shift and flight session was just me cycling through these same thoughts in my head. Eventually, I gave up on clearing my head and shifted back, going into my bedroom and lying in bed until sunrise. The thought of dragging myself through the rest of my day with this weight on my shoulders was miserable, but it had to be done. I'd done it day after day.

Now I skipped breakfast entirely, since even something as simple as that reminded me of Gisela, so I went straight from my bedroom to my headquarters.

The first thing on my agenda was a video call with Simeon about some wolf shifter land that could be sold to us. Good. At least I didn't have to try as hard around him.

I called him over video in my office, sitting back in my office chair.

"Gods, man," Simeon said the moment I picked up. He was at his office back in his headquarters. "What happened?"

"I don't look that bad." The connection slowed and drew out my words. I checked myself on my screen. Fine, I looked rumpled. I fixed my hair. "Okay, I do. Things with Gisela went bad a few days ago."

I explained everything that had happened in as clinical terms as possible. Detaching from the situation was the only way I could get through the story despite the time from the incident. Simeon was uncharacteristically silent, his brow furrowing.

"You know what?" He picked up a notepad covered in writing and held it up. "You have a lot of other shit to worry about, namely the fact that your region is bursting at the seams. Focus on that, not on a woman. Sorry she turned out to be a liar, but you have to focus on what's important."

I clenched my jaw. As pissed off as I was at his casual dismissal of the situation, I didn't blame him. The situation in my region wasn't going to get any better with me moping around. And he had been around the first time this had happened. Throwing myself into my work had gotten me out of my misery, and now I had more than enough to occupy me.

"I know," I finally said. "Let's get started."

We talked about possible areas for wolves to transfer over to dragons for about an hour before hanging up. I scrubbed my hands down my face and looked at the next task. Kai came in with more coffee and lunch, his mouth pressed into a line.

"I'm guessing the briefing for this afternoon isn't positive?" I said, taking the coffee and sandwich from him.

"No, sir. The committee looking into the problems at the local level came back with some disturbing findings. Ryland and May will be here soon to discuss," he said.

"Give me the report now before they arrive."

Kai hesitated, then pulled out his phone to send it to me. When I opened it and skimmed the first page, my eyes widened.

"This is the actual report?" I asked, even though Kai never gave me misinformation.

For a moment, I thought the findings in the report were impossible, but it made sense. Dragon shifters in different territories were banding together to do the exact thing I told them not to: taking over other smaller, weaker dragon packs and beings by force.

"It is, sir. Do you want me to call May and Ryland to get here faster?"

"There's no need," May said, opening the door to my office. "We're here, and we have a lot to discuss."

"This report is a collated version of all the reports you asked Alphas to send after our meeting, plus some new information they gathered," Ryland said.

"Are they all connected, or is this just a natural consequence of all the problems we've been dealing with?" I asked.

"I'm not sure. It seems random. As far as we can tell, their pack members started to organize their efforts independently, and there's not a coordinated attack that we're aware of." May eased into the seat next to me and showed me a map. "The territories shaded in green have information on movements like this popping up, or at least a series of organized crimes that were motivated by territorial disputes.

There could be gaps of unreported crimes, but we can't be sure of that."

The territories in green were spread out with more clusters toward the eastern side of the region.

"There's no pattern that we can see," Ryland said. "Do you see one?"

I studied the map. "No, but it's too much of a coincidence to be popping up in such a small timeframe. They have to be connected. But where's the source? How high does it go?"

"That's where two Alphas near the border of Utah and Arizona come in," Kai said. "They've contacted us saying they arrested a shifter who might know something. Their names are Angelica and Lee. Angelica's pack is larger and attacked Lee's, which is fairly small."

I remembered both of them from the party. The two had been constructive and kind, dedicated to fixing this problem peacefully. And neither of them had given me trouble before—their records were completely clean. I trusted them.

"Did they have any reports of this activity before?" I asked.

"Yes, some." Kai scrolled on his tablet. "They've been dealing with it for a few months."

I drummed my fingers on the table. "Can you brief them on the breadth of the situation so they can work on it as well? I want to go there now and talk to this person they arrested."

"Of course, sir." Kai stood. "And I'll prepare some portals."

"Good." I stood as well. "Let's end this before the violence really begins."

17

GISELA

Stopping in a shifter town wasn't ideal, but we were exhausted, and this town was closest. We had been driving for ten hours non-stop, taking the most roundabout way toward Austin in the hopes of shaking off Zach and Geoffrey. We needed food and rest. Plus, we were sure we hadn't been followed—no one had been behind us for at least forty minutes—so we could probably slow down a bit.

Hailey parked the truck in a lot behind a building, so it wasn't easily visible from the main road, and we walked through the small downtown area.

"I think we passed a diner on our way in," I said. "Want to get some food?"

"Yeah, but look! A hair salon! Want to go in?" She tilted her head toward the salon, which had a big sign in the window that said they accepted walk-ins. "Change up our look?"

"I don't know, Hailey," I said, looking up at the hair salon. "Do you think we have to go this far? Basically getting disguises? Do we have time for this?"

"A haircut might make it easier to blend in. Plus, why not get a fresh start?" She pushed open the door. "Just a small change. We can ask how long it'll take."

A small change. Out of everything we'd been going through, a haircut was no big deal. And if it made us harder to pick out of a crowd, then I was down for it. We didn't feel like Geoffrey and Zach were right on our tail, but it was better to be safe than sorry when it came to our escape.

Hailey and I were able to be seen right away, and the stylists, both of whom were dragon shifters, sat us next to each other.

"What would you like to do today?" My stylist put a cape around my shoulders. "A cut? A color?"

"Color." I was too attached to my hair to chop it all off, even in these circumstances. "Whatever you think would look good."

"I'm ready to chop mine off," Hailey said to her stylist, taking her hair down. "Surprise me."

I raised an eyebrow at her, but she just smiled.

"About how long will it take?" I asked.

"Not too long—we use enchanted color here, so it's much faster than the regular stuff," my stylist said. "Maybe a half hour."

"Perfect."

Our stylists started working on our hair. I loved my hair exactly how it was, and it looked beautiful, too, so I had never been to the salon for more than just a trim or a cut. The stylists and other women in the salon chatted over some pop music playing from a speaker near the front.

"Ugh, my husband, I swear," my stylist said after checking her phone. "Are you married, hon?"

"No."

"Good, stay single." She rolled her eyes.

"Don't scare the poor girl away from love," Hailey's stylist said as she cut an alarming amount of length off Hailey's hair. "What'd he do now?"

"I asked him to be home in time for dinner, but he's going to the tavern to talk about that plan of his." She brushed more color onto my hair. "I'm so tired of him and all this tough talking BS. I just want him to come home at a reasonable hour."

"He and his friends are still going on about those dragon shifters to the west of us?" Hailey's stylist asked.

"Yep." My stylist shook her head and sighed. "Whatever. I'm sick of his nonsense. I doubt it'll work, anyway."

Hailey and I exchanged a look. What was this plan? Dragon shifters were territorial, but we didn't always fight with other packs unless something was wrong. Maybe their conflict was something going back decades.

The stylists talked about other gossip in town—a couple that had accidentally gotten pregnant, a teacher quitting after getting burned out, and a drunken fight at the tavern. Immersing myself in someone else's drama for a while was nice, like watching TV.

If I sat still for too long, I thought about Dex. Or he just barged his way into my thoughts. He loved my hair the way it was, especially when it was spread over his pillows. But he wasn't mine anymore, so what I did with my hair didn't matter at all.

"Okay, all finished," my stylist said, turning me around. "Do you like it?"

She had dyed my hair a strawberry blonde color that went with my complexion more than I thought it would, almost like it was my natural color. I played with the ends, which she had trimmed, too. If Geoffrey or Zach asked around for a dragon shifter with brown hair, people wouldn't think of me.

"It's perfect, thank you."

I admired my hair while Hailey finished up. The stylist had added caramel-colored highlights and cut off a good chunk of her black hair, leaving her with curls that fell just below her chin. The change was drastic, but Hailey clearly loved it.

"It's amazing! I wouldn't have picked this out for myself, but it suits me." She looked at herself from every angle. "Thank you."

"No problem, honey."

We paid and went next door to the diner, settling in a booth in the corner where we could see everything. The restaurant was so small that we couldn't keep our distance from everyone, so this position was good enough.

Each of us ordered a massive meal, since we hadn't eaten in a while, and we weren't sure when we were going to feel safe enough to stop and eat again. Once we were done ordering, I clasped my hands together and rested them between my thighs so I wouldn't fidget with my new hair. Hailey couldn't keep her hands away from hers.

"Want to follow a similar plan as we did last time? Find a place to live, find a job?" Hailey asked. She made a face after tasting her burnt coffee and dumped more sugar in it.

"Yeah, that sounds like a good plan." I glanced over my shoulder when someone sat at the booth behind us. It was just two couples, probably on a double date. "I'm scared about being in the big city. Though I doubt anyone will recognize you with that haircut."

"We'll land on our feet once we find other shifters. I bet there are even more jobs available out there."

And then what? I didn't want to crush Hailey's optimism, so I kept quiet. How many years were we going to have to run from them? Were we going to have to live like this, packing up, moving, and changing our appearances for centuries?

I stirred my coffee, watching the sugar dissolve in the vortex in the middle.

"Yeah, we're moving in soon," the man behind me said. "That pack won't know what hit them."

I stiffened and kept my head down. Hailey must have also heard him because she finally stopped playing with her hair, a crease forming in her brow.

"I don't think you guys should do this," a woman at the table said.

"So what, we're supposed to just sit back and live on top of each other while they have more than enough space? Gods, no." The man behind me laughed. "And it's not like we're the only ones. It's a coordinated thing."

A coordinated attack? That sounded way too much like what I'd overheard at the Alpha dinner back at Dex's. And we were hundreds of miles away from there.

"Coordinated how?" the other woman at the table asked.

"If you came to the meetings, you'd know." The first man shifted in his seat, making the connected booths rock. "It's a movement at this point. I'm excited. What are they going to do, stop all of us at once? First, we take over the weaker dragons, then other weak creatures. Alphas won't have any choice but to use the land if we empty it out."

"It's reckless!" the first woman said. "You can't kill entire packs!"

I dug through my purse and grabbed my phone, typing rapidly in a note. I didn't want evidence of this conversation, just in case things got out of hand and I was roped into whatever crimes were about to happen. *I overheard a conversation like this during the Alpha dinner party. They want to take what's theirs, and I think they're actually doing it.*

I pushed the phone to Hailey, who read the note. Her eyes widened, and she took the phone, typing back: *What?? Dex knows, right?*

He might have known, but he hadn't shared that information with me. I took the phone back and shrugged.

"We should tell him," she said, leaning forward and keeping her voice low. "It sounds like it's going to be big."

I took my phone back and typed another message: *This seems like something an Alpha would stop, right? They're talking about meetings pretty openly. They were talking about it back at the shop.*

Hailey drummed her fingers on the table as she considered what I wrote. Then she took the phone back and typed for a while. Her next message read: *What if Alphas are in on it too? Like some are and some aren't? It's better that we tell him something he already knows than keep this to ourselves and assume he has it under control.*

I bit the inside of my cheek. The thought of going to Dex made me sweat, but this wasn't about us. This was about saving lives.

"I don't know if he'll let me in or hear me out," I whispered. "And what if Geoffrey and Zach are still there waiting?"

"Trust me, I'll make a scene and get us heard, even if it means being thrown in a holding cell." Hailey's green-blue eyes blazed with determination. "We can't sit back and let this happen! We can outrun Geoffrey and Zach."

She was right. And if Dex didn't want to hear me out because of our personal issues, then he wasn't a good Ruler in my book.

"Okay, let's eat and head back to Oregon," I said, my voice steady despite my fear. "We have to get there before anything happens."

18

DEX

I stepped out of the final portal several witches and warlocks had made to connect me from my headquarters near Portland to a small town in southeastern Utah. The witches and warlocks who had opened the portal were there, along with a small cluster of people standing by across the large room.

The dragon shifter I assumed was Angelica stepped forward. She was tall and willowy with a buzzed haircut and green eyes. The male standing next to her must have been Lee. Something about him was undeniably cat-like despite also being a dragon shifter. Members of their council flanked them.

"Thank you for coming on such short notice," Angelica said. "We've been working on making more arrests in connection to the incident."

"How many have you made?" I asked as we walked up the stairs and into Angelica's headquarters.

"Not enough," Lee admitted. "We arrested a dragon shifter from Angelica's pack in the woods after getting a tip that he and several others were going to move in on my pack's land. He's in the holding cell here, but I don't know who else is involved. Clearly, it had to be a lot of people."

"Let me talk to him." I strode faster down the hall behind a guard leading us forward. "Has he confessed anything?"

"Not yet, no," Angelica said, half-jogging to keep up with me. "I haven't told him his punishment yet, which is probably why he hasn't said anything. Not enough pressure. But we did confiscate his phone since we were calling someone over in Alabama when we caught him, talking about a plan."

I was more than happy to apply some pressure.

The holding cell in Angelica's headquarters was just one room with enchanted locks and two guards outside as opposed to my head-quarters' more prison-like space. The dragon shifter, Rafa, was sitting in the corner on the ground, cuffs that kept him from shifting around his wrists.

He stiffened the moment he saw me, averting his eyes.

"Would you like a barrier, sir?" one of the guards asked.

"No need. He's not a threat."

The guards still lingered near me anyway, even as I stepped closer to Rafa's spot on the ground.

I had seen dragon shifters like him time and time again—he was probably all talk, and he always assumed he'd be the biggest, toughest shifter in the room because of his size. And he probably was if he wasn't in the presence of an Alpha or a Ruler. Fighting him wouldn't even count as a warm-up for me.

"Let me hear your side of the story," I said, leaning against the wall adjacent to Rafa. "Try to explain why you were trying to lead a battle against another dragon shifter pack that didn't do anything to you."

He curled his knees up to his chest. "What's my jail time going to look like?"

"It depends on what you tell me and how soon you tell me. The longer you waste the rest of our time, the longer your sentence will be."

The shifter let out a sigh. "I have a child on the way."

"Then you should have thought about that before you got into this." I stepped closer to him, and he flinched.

He rested his head against the wall. "I didn't start this! I'm just one of many."

"We're aware of that at this point. But when you were arrested, you were heard making a phone call to someone." I paced, and every time I came closer to him, he huddled into a smaller ball. "Those records show that you were talking to someone in Alabama about a plan. Who was it?"

"A friend. Distant cousin, actually. This was all his idea." The shifter scoffed. "I should have let him do this first. This was reckless."

"So you're saying this is going to happen in Alabama, too? What's this idea?" I hadn't heard anything from the dragon shifter Ruler in that region, but if this was crossing region lines, I had to get High Ruler Cora and their High Ruler, Filip, involved.

"Yeah. There are more small dragon packs out here, so he figured it was better to consolidate those." The angry edge in his voice encouraged me. The more pissed he was at his alleged friend, the more he'd say.

"What's this man's name?"

"Xander Cane. He's the Alpha of a pack out there, middle of nowhere."

Xander. That name sounded familiar. Where had I heard it?

"Someone tell the team to look into Alpha Xander Cane," I said to one of the guards standing near the door. He hurried off. "He's an Alpha? An Alpha started this movement?"

It made sense. They were the ones who had to deal with their pack's unhappiness on a day-to-day basis, so of course they wanted to do this. Plus, only an Alpha could officially take over another pack, usually by killing the other pack's Alpha. As much as I preached diplomacy, some dragon shifters just weren't going to accept that.

"Yeah, an Alpha. Not everyone who's involved is being directed by an Alpha, like me, but a lot are around here. I don't know who specifically." The shifter shrugged. "Basically, Xander was going to give me the signal to start our attacks on weaker dragon shifter territories. Then I was supposed to give two other people the signal to do the same, and those people would, too, until we covered every group that wanted to be a part of the movement. That's how the idea spread in the first place, so it wasn't anything official. My group jumped the gun because we were excited. Plus, there was an opening. Someone else in my group is probably sending my contact the signal now."

I ground my teeth together and crossed my arms over my chest. Had my meeting backfired? Had I just brought Alphas together to essentially plan a treasonous act that could lead to war?

"We'll find out who. Is that everything you know?" I asked.

"Pretty much. I got the idea from Xander and organized some people in my pack. They told their friends, and it spread from there, all across the region. The seeds of it were already there." He looked up at the ceiling like he hated all of his decisions up until then. "And now I'm here."

I had an ounce of sympathy for the man. His instincts to take territory and protect it weren't his fault. And now he was in jail.

"If you help us connect with Xander, I can give you a lighter sentence," I said.

"Really?" He looked up at me in surprise before averting his gaze. "I'll give you anything you need if I can be out when my child is born."

"When is the baby due?"

"In seven months."

Giving him a seven-month sentence was a joke. "Since no one was hurt or killed, I can give you probation for six months after the child is born. Then, you'll go back to serve the rest of the sentence your Alpha decides."

He rested his forehead on his knees. "Okay."

"Good, come with me."

The guards swooped in right away, flanking the shifter on both sides as we walked to a room that had been converted to a workspace. Ryland, May, and Kai were huddled around a computer, while members of both Angelica's and Lee's councils were working together. The guards sat Rafa on a chair in the corner, standing guard while everyone else worked.

"What have you found about Xander Cane?" I asked over the chatter in the room.

"Here, sir," a woman wearing a baseball cap said, holding up her laptop. "Here's information on him and his pack. They're based in Tipper, Alabama."

I took the laptop and sat down with it, scanning through the file. Whoever this Xander asshole was, he was really good at getting away with a slap on the wrist. Alphas were held to a high standard, just as everyone else was, and anyone could report them for misconduct. If they were reported, the Ruler decided their punishment. Xander's report had several instances of crimes that he had barely been punished for: unfair treatment of female shifters, illegal interrogation tactics, illegal punishments, unpaid labor...

Gods. What a shitbag. He must have been good friends with the previous Ruler to get away with all of this.

But at least the relatively new dragon shifter Ruler in that region, Ilona, was calling him out on it. She had given him his latest reprimand, a fine against his pack, and his record stopped there.

The records got thin in the past thirty or so years since she had been Ruler, so maybe her pressure on him had worked. Or maybe he had flown under the radar if he was behind all of this. I had to find out. His pack was probably miserable with a terrible leader like him. But I wasn't going to step on Ilona's toes.

"Kai, put me in touch with Ilona in the southeastern region," I said.

Kai pulled out his phone and dialed her, handing it over. I cut straight to the point and told her that a dragon shifter in her region was behind a violent movement in mine, and that I needed to step in. Just as Rafa said, no one had started any conflicts there, at least in a coordinated way, so we had to take care of this now. We agreed to meet in her headquarters in an hour.

"Can you text Xander?" I asked Rafa.

"And tell him that I botched the plan?" He scoffed. "Yeah, that'll go well."

"No, just ask him for clarification on it. See if he's at the address we have also. I don't want to go to his pack's town and arouse suspicion if he's hiding out somewhere." I looked around. "Someone bring me Rafa's phone."

Someone handed Kai the phone, and I handed it to Rafa. He still had his enchanted cuffs on, but he was able to hold his phone properly. He let a breath out of his nose and started typing.

"There." He held the phone out to me, and I took it, checking that he'd actually asked for clarification on the plan and where he was before hitting send myself. The response bubbles popped up almost instantly.

Good, let me know when you strike, Xander said. *And I'm at home, what's it to you?*

I handed Kai the phone again and walked toward where the portal was.

"I need portals to Xander's pack's territory. Everyone else wait on standby for my instructions," I said. "We have to end this at the source."

19

GISELA

My heart was in my throat as we sped back toward Oregon. Hailey and I didn't speak much. My head was so filled with thoughts that I didn't know which one to actually say out loud.

Was Dex okay? Were other dragon shifters okay? Nothing like this had ever happened before.

I tried calling Dex again, but no one answered. My texts weren't going through, either, and I wasn't sure if it was our reception or if he had blocked my number.

I rested my head on the window and swallowed hard. What was seeing him again going to be like, especially with these circumstances?

"Shit, we're low on gas," Hailey cursed. "This thing guzzles it like crazy. I'm pulling off the next exit. It looks like there's a lot of stuff there."

"Okay." I checked the time. We had been on the road for five hours already, and we were still so far away. "We have to be quick, though."

Hailey pulled off onto the strip, which was lined with gas stations and fast-food restaurants. The first gas station was relatively empty, so she swung in. I sat there, jiggling my leg as we fueled up, looking at every single car and person in the lot. This was the route we had chosen to avoid the first time, since it was the most logical path to Austin, so Geoffrey and Zach might have been around.

I closed my eyes and rested my head against the seat. The odds of that were low, but they weren't *that* low. By now, they might have known about our new car, and even though it had benefits, it didn't blend as well as a sedan would.

"Okay, we're good to go," Hailey said, hopping back into the driver's seat. "Only two more hours left."

"Two very long hours."

She pulled out onto the street again and sped toward the interstate. Traffic was heavier around here, so several cars got on behind us.

"Can you do me a favor?" Hailey asked. Her grip on the steering wheel was so hard that her knuckles were white. "Keep an eye on that gray car behind us through the mirror on your side."

"Are we being followed?" I looked in the mirror. The car was in the lane to our right, a comfortable distance away.

"I don't know, but he's been behind us for a while." Hailey drummed her fingers on the steering wheel, checking the rearview mirror. "I might be paranoid, honestly."

"Better paranoid than dead."

I kept my eyes locked on the mirror. Its presence didn't worry me at first, but as we got further away from the area where we'd gotten gas and more into a rural area, my worry increased.

"I think he's following us," I said, slouching down in my seat. "Wouldn't he have passed us by now if he were just a regular car?"

Hailey braked, her eyes going between the mirror and the road in front of her. The car behind us didn't pass us. And when we sped up, they sped up, too. Shit.

"Okay, how did they find us, and what do we do now?" I asked.

"First of all, we take some deep breaths and try not to panic." Hailey kept her eyes on the road and pressed the accelerator harder, making the engine rumble louder. "I think we should keep going. It'll be safer if we're near the headquarters. Or if we can't make it that far, there's some other shifter towns nearby, I think."

I watched the car in the window, my hands shaking so badly that I sat on them to stop myself. It didn't work.

Shifter and other magical being towns didn't just appear out of thin air—signs that were glamoured so humans couldn't see them lined the sides of the interstate. A shifter town called Marlborough was only five miles away.

"Want to stop here and ask for help?" Hailey asked. "It's kind of the middle of nowhere..."

"It's something. Let's do it."

She switched lanes in front of the car following us and slammed the accelerator down, pressing me back to my seat. The car behind us sped up, confirming our worst suspicions. Hailey was going so fast that I worried we'd fly off the road, especially when we had to make a turn on a dirt one to get to this town.

The gray car was right on our tail, almost ramming into us. Hailey swerved, narrowly missing a ditch, and pulled back onto the road. The top of my head hit the car ceiling as we rode over a huge root sticking up the road and bounced back down. One of our tires made a sickening thumping sound and keeled to the right.

"Did we blow up a tire? Is that possible?" Hailey asked, trying to compensate for the car's rapidly deflating tire. "What's the point of having a truck if it can't go over obstacles?"

"Watch out, there's another one!"

It was too late—we ran over another root, and the tire blew, sending us swerving back and forth across the narrow dirt road. Hailey and I screamed as the truck caught a rock in the ditch and flipped onto it, rolling to its bottom. My whole body rocked back and forth, getting slammed into the shattered glass, my seat, and the airbag. We turned so many times that I was dizzy, which didn't help my throbbing head. Finally, we came to a stop upside down at the bottom.

"Are you okay?" Hailey asked.

"I think so." I touched my forehead and came away with blood. "We should—"

A pair of denim-clad legs appeared next to my window, and the man attached to them wrenched the car door off. He sliced through my seatbelt and grabbed me by the hair, dragging me outside.

"There you are, you sneaky bitch," Zach snarled, pulling me along. I screamed as loudly as I could, but we were truly in the middle of nowhere. No one was driving by or coming in and out of the town that was allegedly at the end of this road. "You thought you could get away with this? With some hair dye and a different car?"

"Hailey, run!" I shouted. "Get out of here!"

"She shouldn't bother. We have eyes all over the place. Why the fuck did you come back this way?" He laughed, gripping my hair tighter.

I kicked and grabbed his wrist, trying to get my feet under me as he pulled me up the slope of the ditch. It was no use. I was strong in my human form, but not nearly as strong as he was. I shifted into my dragon form, the pain of my injuries from the accident fading into the back of my mind. Hailey had done the same thing and was zooming upwards and away. Why wasn't Geoffrey chasing her down? He threw something at her like a lasso, swearing when he missed.

I stretched my wings and flew up. My dragon was small but speedy, so I had to get a head start to possibly get away.

Something wrapped around my foot, and the breath left my body, my entire view shifting back to that of my human form in the blink of an eye. I looked down at myself. I was a hundred feet in the air in my human form, some sort of gold lasso around my ankle.

And I was falling. Fast.

I tried my hardest to shift again, but it was like slamming my body into a brick wall. This was it. They were just going to kill me here instead of taking me back to Xander?

"There we go," Zach said, catching me with ease. "Glad this worked."

The rope around my ankle glowed. It must have been enchanted to stop me from shifting. My power leeched from my body, but I still tried to fight. I refused to go back. My fate was probably even worse than I could have ever imagined before all of this. Was Xander going to kill me himself? Clip my wings so I could never fly again? Or something even worse?

Zach threw me in the trunk of the car, stuffing my mouth with a cloth and taping it shut. Then, he shut the trunk. My entire body trembled. How was I supposed to get out of this? I struggled against my bonds, but the more I did, the weaker I got, like someone had poked a hole in my energy supply and let it drain out.

Tears leaked out of my eyes as the car started again.

"The other one got away," Geoffrey said from outside of the car. The driver's side dipped down, and the door shut.

At least Hailey had gotten free. If anyone could find help, it was her.

I just hoped she could track someone down in time.

20

———

DEX

"Can't we get more witches or warlocks to put together this portal?" I barked.

Five were already there, trying to create one that went as long a distance as possible. From there, they had to make another one to get me to where Xander was, since going from eastern Utah all the way to Alabama in one stretch was too much for some of the strongest witches we had at our disposal.

It was a magically intensive process and took time, but I wanted to arrest Xander now and cut off this movement at the source. He didn't deserve to be an Alpha. Most of my pack and council trickled through the initial portals I had taken from Oregon to eastern Utah, just in case there was a fight. Xander wasn't known for playing fair, and we weren't sure if he was alone.

"We're trying our best, sir," the lead witch said, turning her attention back to the spell.

I raked my hand through my hair and paced more. To make matters worse, Ilona had been visiting a friend in south Texas, so she was trying to get her portals to the town ready. High Ruler Filip was up north in New York City, too, so it was going to take him a while to get there also.

"I don't think Xander will strike, sir. He doesn't know that we're onto him," Kai murmured to me. "I've instructed everyone to hurry with finding and arresting the rebellious groups."

"But the more uprisings we stop, the more likely it is that he'll hear about them. We need to hurry before he tries to run." I stopped when a commotion came up near the portal my pack was steadily coming through.

"Move, please! I need to speak to Ruler Dex—Dexter, I mean!" It took me a moment to recognize her with shorter hair, but it was Hailey. She barreled through the crowd in the large room, looking worse for wear. Her clothes were torn, and she had a deep, fresh gash across her forehead. "Sir, I need to talk to you! It's extremely important! I know that things were bad with...you know, that thing, but this is worse!"

Her rumpled appearance, the desperation in her eyes, and her pleading were enough to sway me.

"Fine." I walked into the hallway, and she followed. "What happened to you?"

"Gisela was taken! By Xander!" she blurted once we were away from the door. "And—"

"Wait, what?" I held up my hand. "Xander Cane, of Tipper, Alabama?"

"Yeah! How do you know him?" Hailey asked.

I ignored her, my heart pounding. "How does Gisela know him?"

Hailey blinked. "Because he's our pack's Alpha? The pack we left."

The breath left my lungs in a gust. "*What?*"

The meeting with Geoffrey and Zach came flooding back into my head.

I doubt you mentioned that you've cheated on Xander in the past.

Xander will be excited to see you.

"Okay, hold on." Hailey put one hand on her hip. "She didn't tell you this?"

"She told me that her fiancé was her pack's Alpha, and that he wasn't a good being." I leaned against the wall of the hallway. My world had turned sideways.

When Geoffrey and Zach came... That was where I heard Xander's name! But all I had been able to focus on was the fact that Gisela had lied to me, and so I had pushed away everything else that had happened during that meeting. And even though she had said she had done it for good reasons, that hadn't swayed me. Just because I didn't have hard proof that she had broken up with him, but the others did.

The lie did hurt, but now she was in danger because I had let my past and my fear blind me. I hadn't trusted her, even though, until that point, she hadn't done anything for me *not* to trust her.

There wasn't enough air in the hallway, but I couldn't leave. My feet were frozen in place. How could I have done this?

"Well, he took her! More specifically, the two guys who showed up at your house chased us off the road, tied Gisela up with some rope that prevented her from shifting, and took her away! I was able to get away and flew to your headquarters. Someone told me you were here, and I snuck through the portal." Hailey leaned against the wall, too, gasping for air.

"When did all of this happen?" I asked, a surge of fear unlike anything I'd ever felt before flowing through my veins.

"A couple of hours ago. But the other important thing is that dragon shifters are planning an uprising or something! Trying to take over smaller dragon packs?" Hailey craned her neck to look back into the room she had burst into. "Though I'm guessing that you guys have figured that out."

"Now that's my second priority. The first is finding Gisela," I said. "Finding her means finding Xander, and we already know where he is."

"If he has any idea that people are coming, he'll run," Hailey warned me.

"I know. That's why we're trying to hurry." I looked at my watch and went back into the room. "Come on, we're leaving."

"We? Wait, what's happening? What's the plan?" Hailey jogged to catch up with me.

"We're going to go in and get Gisela, then we're going to stop

Xander from spreading this attack in this region. The fucking coward couldn't start the chaos in his own region first. He was probably going to pretend he had nothing to do with it if it failed," I snarled, barely able to keep the venom out of my voice.

I wanted to rip Xander limb from limb. It would be a more efficient solution—I could get back at him for hurting Gisela and for organizing this chain reaction of a rebellion. He was going to be put to death for this, anyway.

But I couldn't do that, at least not yet.

"I'll help! I'm not very big as a dragon, but I'm scrappy!" Hailey said, standing strong. "I can't let him hurt Gisela, either. I've been by her side this entire time."

She shot a sidelong glance at me that I should have reprimanded her for. But she was absolutely right. I had betrayed the woman I loved.

"Once we find Gisela, I'm going to make it up to her," I murmured to Hailey. "I'll grovel for decades if it means having her back."

She blinked. "You mean that?"

"I swear my life on it."

"Wow." Hailey shook her head and laughed. "I believe you. She's pissed, but she misses you, even if she's not saying it all the time."

The weight on my shoulders lightened. "Really?"

"Really."

"The portals are ready, sir!" a witch called.

"Let's go," I said. "Everyone fall behind me and stay back. Stay hidden. I'll give you the signal if I need backup."

I ran through the first portal, more determined than I'd ever been in my life to succeed. The witches and warlocks had opened portals all the way to Alabama, separated between several feet at each stop. The weather was drastically different in each destination until we reached Alabama, which was hot and so humid that my shirt stuck to my body immediately.

The portal had put us out in the woods about a mile away from Xander's address. It was clear, so I signaled for those in the other section of the portal to come through.

"Some of you stay back here," I said, gesturing to half of those who had followed me through. "The others find hiding spots."

Everyone followed my orders, but Hailey stuck to my side.

"I have to stick with you. I don't know if I can sit this one out," she said. "Front lines or nothing."

"Okay. Stick close to me, then, and follow my lead." I glanced at her. She looked like she had been through a lot today. "And if I tell you to leave, then leave. Got it?"

She nodded.

We walked through the woods, and I scented the air, trying to figure out if we were alone or not. The air smelled suspiciously like forest and only forest. No shifters.

"So what are we doing?" Hailey asked once the town came into view.

"We're going to see if Xander is at his house. It doesn't seem like people are here." I smelled the air now that the wind had changed direction and caught the scent of a few shifters. "A few are here, but it shouldn't be a battle."

"Shouldn't be?"

"You're with me. I can take out a small, backwater pack," I said before remembering that she had come from here. "Not that you're—"

"No, you're right. They won't know what's hit them."

We went silent again and crept out into town, sticking to perimeters before going closer and closer into the center of town. I didn't smell Gisela, but that didn't mean she was gone. Maybe they were masking her scent somehow. I wasn't giving up hope.

Xander's home was the biggest in town, though they were all fairly modest. A guard stood out front, looking at his phone. I held up a hand to tell Hailey to stay put in the bushes. Then, I sprinted up to him from behind and dragged him to the side of the house, my hand over his mouth. He squirmed in protest, but he wasn't nearly as strong as me.

"I'm going to move my hand, but you're not going yell. There's something in this for you," I whispered in his ear. "Understood?"

He shook his head once, and I removed my hand.

"I swear, I'm just a guard!" the man said quietly, putting his hands out in front of him. "I'm not holding anyone hostage!"

I raised an eyebrow. "Okay...I wasn't insinuating that you were. I need to know where Xander is."

"I'm not supposed to tell you."

"Is he inside the house? Is anyone else inside the house?" My patience was running thin already.

"N-no," he stammered. I gripped his shirt. "What do I get if I tell you?"

"Your life, first of all," I said. I wasn't going to kill him, but he blanched anyway. "And I'll arrange for you get a lesser punishment when all of this collapses."

"Good enough for me," he murmured. "He's at his bunker for some reason with the rest of the pack."

"His bunker? What made him run?"

"Don't know, but it seems like he was meeting someone there?" He shrugged. "Clearly, I'm at the bottom of the totem pole if I'm doing this!"

Meeting someone—maybe Gisela? I looked over at the bushes where Hailey was waiting. We had to check it out. I didn't want to miss Gisela if she was there.

I shook him in frustration. "Tell me where it is, right now! Is there anyone here who could tail us there?"

"No, not really! People might be around, but if you move quietly, they might not see you. But there might be people around the bunker!" The man held his hands up in front of his face. "Listen, I'll tell you where to go! Just don't hurt me!"

He gave me the directions to the bunker. Once he had served his purpose, I dropped him and waved to Hailey. I wasn't sure if we were going to find Gisela there, but we had to try.

"Hailey, go tell everyone that I need backup. We're going to get Xander at his bunker."

And, hopefully Gisela.

21

GISELA

I was shut in the trunk for what felt like hours but was probably only one. Geoffrey didn't care that I was back here, alive, because he hit every bump, slammed his brakes, and swerved. I rolled around the back like luggage until I gathered the strength to get this awful rope off of me. It drained me almost entirely, but I did it.

Not being able to see out of the trunk was unnerving, especially since I heard trucks zooming by and honking. Was it still day? Was I going to be stuck here all the way back to Alabama? The thought of that made my already exhausted body even weaker.

We slowed down and rolled to a stop on another gravel or dirt road from the feel of it. Geoffrey and Zach got out of the car, popping the trunk. It was dusk, and we were in the middle of another forest.

"Shit, she came untied," Zach said, grabbing the rope I'd gotten out of and retying my wrists. "You sure this is legit enchanted to make her weaker and not shift?"

"Of course it is. I mean, look at her. She's basically dead, and she didn't shift." Geoffrey laughed as if I wasn't there. Gods, I hated him. "It was worth every penny."

Where did they even find something like that? And how long had they been searching for me if they had gone out of their way to get it?

Zach picked me up and threw me over his shoulder. I turned so I could see where we were going. A man—a warlock—was standing next to an open portal, which opened to another portal. My eyes widened.

"Here you go," Geoffrey said, handing the warlock an enormous wad of cash. "As promised."

"Let me count it," the warlock said, glancing at me. I hid my face again.

"Come on, man. We have to get her back," Zach said.

The warlock ignored him, going quiet for a while. "Fine, you can go."

Zach and Geoffrey didn't thank him as they walked through the portal. The new place we were in was raining, but we weren't there for long. From there, we went through two more portals and ended up in a familiar forest. Our hunting grounds back in Alabama.

I'd regained some strength, so I tried to wiggle free, as if I could escape two strong shifters all tied up. Zach smacked the back of my leg, hard, but lost his hold on me as he did. I fell with a thump, my head hitting the ground.

"Bro, be careful, for fuck's sake! You can't just drop her," Geoffrey said, picking me up this time.

"I know." Zach tightened up my bindings again, their enchantment sucking my energy away.

We walked into the woods for a half hour or more. If we were flying, it probably would have taken five minutes, so it felt extra long. Eventually, we stopped, and Zach opened what sounded like a heavy door. It was built into the ground, which we descended under. Then, there was a hallway and another set of stairs to an empty concrete room with a chair in it.

Geoffrey dumped me in the chair and repurposed my ties, so I was attached to it. To my surprise, he peeled off the tape on my mouth next. I spat out the cloth and screamed at the top of my lungs.

"Gods, shut the fuck up!" Geoffrey hissed, getting in my face. "No one can hear you down here. You really think we'd let your mouth free if anyone could?"

He had a point. My head dipped. Was I going to be able to get out of here? My hope slipped by the minute.

"Should we give her water or something?" Zach asked.

"Please," I whispered.

"Sure, I guess. Wouldn't want her to black out or anything." Geoffrey looked at me, then went over to a cabinet on the far side of the room. The water bottle he had in his hand was like seeing an oasis.

He uncapped it and pushed it into my mouth, tilting the bottle so I had to guzzle it down. It tasted like someone had left the bottle in a hot car for weeks, but it was better than nothing. I gasped for air after it was empty.

Geoffrey tossed the water bottle on the floor and looked down at me. I hated how closely we resembled each other, even with my new hair.

"Why'd you bother trying to get away?" he asked, circling me with slow, steady steps. "Were you going to fight us off? You small, pathetic female?"

I refused to look at him and give him the satisfaction of having him attention. The words hit deeper than they had when I was with the pack. After being in a place where I was actually respected, being associated with being weak just because I was a female was a massive change.

"What was with that Ruler, by the way? You lived with him?" Zach frowned, standing directly in front of me. Then, a realization lit up his face. "Were you fucking him for money on the side? I bet you were."

I shook my head. "I didn't do that."

"Nah, I bet you did." Geoffrey stopped and grabbed my chin, forcing me to look into his cold brown eyes. "Now you're damaged goods. Xander won't like that one bit."

Zach ran his finger down the side of my neck, making me shudder. "Gorgeous but boring. And stupid, apparently, for running from a marriage to an Alpha. You had your whole life set up, and you threw it away to become a cook? So stupid."

I growled despite myself, making them both laugh.

"You couldn't have just stayed here and served Xander instead? Gotten knocked up and helped us take over all these weak packs sucking up resources?" Geoffrey squatted down so we were almost eye to eye.

Hailey's spirit must have taken over me, because I impulsively spat in his face. Geoffrey reeled back in shock, then got a hold of himself. His slap made my whole body rock and my face sting.

"Disgusting." Geoffrey wiped off his face and stood, stalking away from me. "I swear, I should kill you now and save Xander a few—"

"Don't touch her." Xander appeared at the bottom of the stairs, alone. "She's mine."

My body trembled as hard as I tried to keep still. Xander's face was friendly and calm, which was far worse than his normal anger. It just meant that he was about to go ballistic.

"My beautiful Gisela." He smiled, slinking toward me. "You look worse for wear."

He cupped my face with his hand and made me look up at him. I met his gaze with a sharp stare that was far too defiant. But he wasn't my Alpha anymore, and he wasn't deserving of the title. He ran his thumb across my cheek in a motion that reminded me of Dex, but in some dark, alternate universe. I shuddered.

"What, you don't want your fiancé's touch?" Xander asked. "We can be married by the end of the day."

"She's used goods," Geoffrey said, his arms crossed over her chest. "She was living with the Ruler over in Oregon."

Xander's face went blank, and I braced myself for his explosion. His hand gripped my face even tighter, and he got so close to me that I flinched back.

"Were you really, Gisela? Did you have the audacity to try to end this engagement with a damn text message, then sleep with another man?" Xander shouted inches from my face. I shook so badly that my words stayed trapped in my throat. "Tell me!"

"Y-yes."

He swore and pushed my face away, stalking around the room. If there were furniture in here besides this chair, he would have thrown it. Instead, he put his fist through a concrete wall.

"Damn it, Gisela! I was going to be merciful and let you marry me since I assumed you were young and dumb. But now you're damaged," Xander hissed. "Gods, how dare you let another man touch you? You were *mine*! The engagement could never end unless *I* said it did!"

I choked back tears, though one slipped out. Xander went on a rampage, ripping the doors off of the cabinets and throwing them, narrowly missing me.

"I need to think of what to do with you next," he panted, his breathing heavy. "The punishment needs to fit the crime. Geoffrey, Zach, let's go."

Xander stormed up the stairs with Geoffrey and Zach behind him. The door at the top of the stairs slammed, then the door at the end of the hallway did, too. The room plunged into darkness not long after.

I hyperventilated for a few seconds, shaking so hard the chair creaked. Was he leaving to get tools to torture me? Or was he just thinking of the best way to do it to punish me? Or worse, what if he just killed me? Or made me his slave, unable to shift ever again?

I had to get out of here. Hailey might have gotten help or come looking for me.

Thoughts of Dex popped into my head. I wanted that safe feeling he'd given me. But now I had to create that feeling on my own.

The ropes around my wrist had drained my energy and some of my dragon senses, so it took me a while to adjust to the darkness. Once my night vision was back, I tested the ropes around my wrist. They were tight, but there was a sharp corner on the back of the chair, maybe from where it had been put together incorrectly.

Little by little, I rubbed the rope against that sharp edge. I stopped, taking breaks, but kept forging on. I gasped when the rope finally tore, freeing my hands. I undid the ones at my ankles, which had dug into my skin to the point where it was rubbed raw, and stood.

My legs buckled underneath me, and I grabbed the chair. How many hours had it been since I'd stood on my own two feet? I stretched and let the blood flow back into them before I implemented my plan. I pulled off a metal piece of the chair, hoping I could use it to break open a lock or stab someone.

I took off my shoes to quiet my footsteps and inched toward where I remembered the stairs being. I groped the wall until I felt the opening, then crawled up the stairs. The light in the hallway above was off, too, which was good and bad. I still had the cover of darkness, and they were probably gone, but I didn't know what waited for me up there. I hadn't taken in as many details of the space.

I made it to the top of the stairs and took a deep breath, preparing myself to break open the lock. To my surprise, they'd done the work for me. It was unlocked.

I paused, letting the door drift open. Was this just a mistake, or was Xander luring me into a trap? I crawled on my hands and knees along the wall, my heart pounding with every sound I thought I heard. Was I going the right way? The hallway was long on both sides, very faint light under both. I made it to one and stopped before I tried the next door, making contingency plans.

What if I tripped an alarm? I'd try to shift and fly away. But what if there was a spell on this area? Then... Well, I wasn't sure. Best case scenario, they had left this place unguarded, assuming I'd never get out, or if they did have guards, they were sleeping on the job.

I tested the lock, and again, it was open. This had to be a trap. I was going to trip an alarm, or someone was going to grab me by the ankle and drag me downstairs once more.

But light poured through the space below the door, like it led to the stairs that we'd come down from outside. I had to try.

I pushed open the door and found myself in the woods already at a different entry to the dungeon. I froze. No alarms. No arrows flying at me. No guards from what I could see.

I ran. My legs were still so weak that I was hobbling along, but I was getting away from that hell hole. I tripped over a branch and tumbled to the ground. An alarm beeped in the distance. Shit.

I pushed myself to my feet again and tried to run forward. The trees were thick around here, so I wedged myself through them until I was in an area where I could possibly fly. Men's shouting echoed behind me, way closer than I was comfortable with. I grunted and tried to shift mid-run, but my body didn't cooperate.

"Come on, come on!" I chanted to myself as I tried again and again. Then, on my third try, I shifted.

I fluttered above the ground like a chicken, my wings too weak to propel me upward. I was too far in now to stop, so I jumped up some sturdy branches to get some height before taking off. The men had shifted, too, their wings whooshing behind me as they caught up. I darted down, weaving through a thatch of close-together trees that they couldn't fit through.

Loud crashes and angry roars rang through the woods behind me. When I looked back, they weren't on my tail anymore. Yes! The small win boosted my strength, pushing me to new heights. When I reached a clearing, I flew up to get a better view of where I was. Our town was far off in the distance, a small cluster of lights tucked into the woods.

I didn't get to see the rest of the view because someone slammed into me, hard, knocking me out of the air and into the trees. I hit them so hard that they splintered, and my breath left my lungs.

A female shifter I didn't recognize hovered over me, smoke floating out of her nose before she dive-bombed me. I tried to blow fire at her, but she was too fast, ramming into me and biting down on my neck. I growled, scratching at her, but I was just too exhausted to get anywhere.

A male shifter with reddish scales landed and shifted back to his human form—it was Zach. He took more of that rope he had bound me with out of a sealed pouch he'd carried around his neck and tied it around one of my ankles. I cried out in pain as my body contracted back into its human form.

"Gods, you're a pain in the ass," Zach said, tying me up so tightly that my circulation was cut off in my ankles and wrists. "Come on. I'm fed up with carrying you around."

Instead of picking me up, he wrapped my hair around his wrist and pulled me along. I was so worn out that I let it happen, even though it hurt. It was nothing compared to what was waiting for me. I let the tears I'd been holding back fall.

The pain in my scalp suddenly stopped, and Zach just...disappeared. I looked up and saw him hurtling across the sky, thrown by the massive, black-scaled dragon that was hovering over me.

I hadn't seen him in his dragon form before, but my heart knew it was Dex.

He had come for me.

The most overwhelming rush of love tore through me, opening my soul. It was like someone had snapped together two puzzle pieces between us, filling a gap that had been dying to be filled. A flood of emotions came over me, too, mostly joy.

Our mate bond.

22

DEX

I felt everything—Gisela's fear, her happiness, her love for me, her relief. It was the most beautiful thing I'd ever experienced. I had never felt anything so potent, yet so natural, like we were supposed to be together all this time, but we had to wait for the perfect moment.

She was my mate, and she was alive.

I shifted back into my human form and fell to my knees, cradling Gisela in my trembling arms.

"I've got you," I said, undoing the ropes. They stung against my skin, like a minor bug bite, but I felt they were hurting her through our bond. Once they were off, I balled them up and burned them in my fists. "Gisela, are you all right?"

I brushed her hair out of her face. Gods, she had been through a lot. She had half-healed cuts on her face, a fresh bruise on her cheek, and scratches all over. But she was alive and breathing. I tried to focus on that instead of my murderous rage at the men who had hurt her. She was already terrified enough.

"You found me," she rasped.

"I did." I brushed her hair out of her face, holding her close. I kissed her as softly as I could since her lip had split.

Her eyelids fluttered closed, and she relaxed in my arms. She was fast asleep. I stood up with her in my arms and walked toward the edge of the clearing. Finding her was lucky. After we stormed Xander's house and got the information about where he was from the easily manipulated guard, my pack and council flew to find this underground bunker he had in the middle of the woods. But Gisela had escaped.

I scented her and her blood in the air and found her just in time. That female shifter probably would have tried to kill her if Zach hadn't appeared. And he might have killed her himself if he had been reckless enough with her.

Even though she was asleep, I said, "I'm taking you to a safe place, beautiful. Keep resting."

Her eyes opened for a moment before she fell asleep again. It was easier to move her this way, at least. I carried her toward the kit I'd dropped closer to the underground bunker, unable to take my eyes off of her. Seeing her again, so battered but still pushing forward, was too much to handle. I gripped her tighter. She was alive. And once a healer got to her, she would be healthy.

I found the pack and unfolded a huge bag, tucking Gisela inside of it. It was easier to carry her like this in my dragon form so my talons wouldn't pierce her skin. I had to take her back to the portal and put her through it before coming back to find Xander. Her safety was my biggest priority.

I shifted back into my dragon form and gathered up the bag Gisela was in, carefully ascending above the trees so she wouldn't hit any branches. Hailey was waiting near the bunker in her human form, pacing back and forth. I landed so she could at least see Gisela was safe.

"She's okay? Is she okay?" Hailey asked as I landed. She pulled open the sides of the bag and gasped. "Woah, wait. Are you two mates?"

"Yes, we are." A swell of protectiveness came over me, even though Hailey wasn't a threat.

"I wish she were awake so I could properly congratulate her."

She hugged Gisela as much as she could while Gisela was in the bag, but their reunion was short-lived. I heard rustling hundreds of yards away. Everyone was supposed to stay near town and not leave, so it wasn't any of us.

My blood boiled, and I shifted, smoke blowing out of my nose. Hailey soon heard them and shifted into her dragon form as well.

Take her back to town. I'll fight them off, I told her telepathically. I didn't like the idea of Gisela not being near me, but I trusted Hailey. I needed to express some of the rage that was building up inside of me, preferably by beating the shit out of anyone who had laid a finger on her. No one was going to hurt my mate ever again.

Hailey did as I said, gathering her best friend and taking flight. I flew alongside them, and when we cleared the tops of the trees, we saw how close the pack was. At least there were only five of them.

I urged Hailey forward, and she zoomed off, keeping as low as she could. One dragon from the pack peeled off, going for her, so I attacked him first. He wasn't going to get anywhere near Gisela. I was much, much faster than a regular dragon ever could be, so I smashed into him talons first before he knew what was happening.

We rolled through the air, the other dragon roaring and trying to blast me with fire. What a waste of it. I was impervious to a regular dragon's fire, but mine ran much, much hotter than theirs. I torched his wing and let him go, sending him spiraling and unable to right himself.

I didn't have time to celebrate. The four remaining dragons of the pack descended on me all at once, biting and clawing me, and Hailey wasn't completely in the clear yet. Four against one was a much fairer fight, but it was still in my favor. I ducked and dove, speeding around them and taking shots at their wings. I was much nimbler than they were, flying circles around them and making them crash into each other.

Once they were tangled up and disoriented, I took out their wings one by one until all of them had fallen through the canopy of trees below.

Easy.

I hovered above the trees, sensing if anyone else was coming. I was alone again, so I made a loop and went back toward town and the final leg of the portal as fast as my wings could carry me.

Gisela was waiting for me. I needed her more than I needed to breathe. She was my greatest motivation.

I heard the commotion well before I saw it. Something was on fire, and from the scents beneath the smoke, it was the town I had just left. I sped up and soared above the scene. Part of my pack had already shifted, hovering above the ground across from Xander's pack. This match wasn't even, at least numbers-wise. Almost everyone else was miles away, closer to the portal.

They stopped fighting as I flew overhead. Buildings had gotten caught in the conflict, burning brightly and blown to pieces from dragons smashing themselves or objects into them mid-fight. I didn't want collateral damage like that, but at least we got the innocent members of the pack out of town.

There he is, a man's voice echoed through my head. *Just the man I want to tear to shreds!*

I landed in the middle of the two sides, spreading my wings. A greenish brown dragon drifted forward and growled at me.

Xander, I'm assuming, I said into his mind.

And you're the man who tainted Gisela.

Tainted? He seriously thought I had tainted her? Rage pumped through my veins. She was an object to him. I could have replaced Gisela's name with anything, and the meaning would have been the same.

Xander feinted toward me, and I dodged him with ease.

You're really going to try me? I asked with a snort, smoke floating from my nostrils.

He didn't respond—he tried to take a dirty hit, swiping at my eyes. I dodged him again and head butted him several feet backwards. His pack shifted into formation behind him.

I have my entire pack. Who do you have? Xander asked.

I blew a flare of white-hot fire straight up into the air, the signal that my backup had been waiting for. Xander froze but quickly recovered, taking another swipe at me. This time, his pack joined in. Four normal shifters was easy, but thirty normal shifters and an Alpha was a little much, even for me.

I dipped and dodged the dragons as much as I could, willing backup to get here already. Finally, a wolf howled beneath me, and several others joined in. I did a barrel roll to get away from another dragon, putting him just low enough for a wolf shifter to jump up the side of a building and launch himself at him.

The wolf latched onto the dragon's foot, shaking him so hard that the dragon couldn't maintain flight. I led the other dragons in Xander's pack that were following me downward into jumping distance of High Ruler Filip's army of shifters and other magical beings, which filtered in through the woods. Xander's idiots finally realized what was happening and flew back up, only to be met with my pack and Ilona's, with Ilona at the front.

Xander's pack hesitated for a second, but they valiantly tried despite being outnumbered. The two groups clashed, and I flew upward, feeling Xander on my tail. He was much faster than I thought he would be, but not faster than me. Of course, he took a dirty shot at me and bit my tail, trying to drag me down with him.

You asshole! Xander cried. *Who do you think you are, attacking my pack?*

If I were in my human form, I would have laughed. Who did he think *he* was? This fight was absurd, and his men were being pummeled, but he kept trying. And he kept trying for me.

All this fighting over a worthless excuse for a woman! Xander added, trying to drag me down again.

I snapped instantly, blowing white hot fire directly into his face. He roared, falling and clawing at his face.

Never speak of Gisela again, I ordered, dive-bombing him and sending us shooting toward the ground. He slammed into it, digging a crater into a clearing. My blood was boiling, and my body didn't feel like my own. I had thought about ripping him limb from limb in a hyperbolic sense before, but now? Now I wanted to make it a reality.

I clamped down onto his neck with my mouth and grabbed one

of his wings with my claws. With a violent pull, I yanked his wing off, splitting him open and killing him instantly. The man who had terrorized my mate was dead, and I was proud to be the one who had done it.

I shifted back into my human form, my chest heaving. The battle around me was basically over, with my side having won readily.

Filip's massive wolf form strolled up to me, licking blood off his chops. He shifted back into his human form, glancing over his shoulder at Xander's corpse and shrugging.

"That was ridiculous, wasn't it?" Filip said. "They really tried as if they could win. This backward pack from the middle of nowhere."

"I know. But there was a lot of rage there." I looked down at Xander's body. I laughed, though I was so mentally and emotionally exhausted that it sounded hysterical.

"You should get back to Gisela. And maybe take a nap or something so you don't let out that psychotic laugh again." Filip clapped me on the shoulder. "Nice battle."

I brushed soot and dirt off of my hands and checked on everyone before going to where I belonged—by Gisela's side.

23

———

GISELA

Everything hurt, but in a different way than it did when I was in that car crash, or dragged by my hair, or tied up in the trunk of a car, or magically drained by enchanted rope.

Gods, I had been through it in the past few days.

Now the pain was the dull ache of healing—snug bandages and stitched up gashes, plus a dull headache that got worse when the healer turned on the light.

I shielded my eyes with my hand and groaned. I was in Dex's bed, a pile of pillows behind me. Dex's scent permeated the room, taking the edge off my anxiety.

"Sorry, hon," the soft-spoken warlock healer said, putting a hand on my shoulder. "Just need to give you more of this tincture. Open."

I opened my mouth, and he squirted a droplet of a tincture under my tongue. It tasted horrendous, like fish sauce mixed with strawberries of all things. I gagged.

"Have I been given this before?" I asked, reaching for the cup of water on the side table. I winced as it pulled on a bruise I had.

"Yes, but we put you in an unconscious state while we healed the worst of your wounds." The nurse handed me the cup. "You've been in and out for a while."

My headache melted away almost immediately. "Wow, that stuff tastes awful, but it works."

"It does." The warlock hovered his hands over my body, his face going serious in his concentration. After a few moments, he nodded and smiled. "You're healing up well. I think you might be ready for visitors if you're up for it. You have a few people waiting."

"Who's out there?"

"Your best friend has been very insistent on being first." He chuckled. "But Ruler Dexter is on his way. He's needed to tie up a lot of loose ends."

Dex. Memories of our mate bond snapping into place were vivid in my mind, but I also faintly remembered him untying me, cradling me in his arms with pure worry across his handsome features. My heart leapt into my throat. That look and the feeling pulsing through our bond said more words than a simple apology would have. We had so much to talk about, though, and Hailey was probably losing it.

"Send Hailey in, please."

The healer nodded and left. The door opened, and fast footsteps approached. Hailey threw open the curtain and flung herself at me.

"Gisela, oh, gods, you're okay!" She gave me a squeeze that was too much for my body, and I groaned. "Sorry! You look so much better than you did before!"

"So do you." The last memory I had of her was when we were in the overturned car, and she was bleeding from a gash on her forehead. Now she just had a faint scar.

"You feel different, too, now that you're mates," Hailey said with a grin. "Congrats."

"Thank you. I can hardly believe it." I reached into myself and felt Dex. His mind was busy, and a lot was on his plate. "What happened besides that?"

"So, so much." She sat down in the seat next to my bed and sighed. "But it's still going on, I think."

"They're still fighting?"

"No, they're still trying to get a grip on those uprisings before they happen. But besides that, I don't know the details. I just flew you from where Dex dropped you off to the portal."

I sat back in my bed, the fluffy pillows dipping inward with my weight.

"So it's over?" I asked. "I'm...Xander is..."

"He's gone. He's dead. Dex killed him."

Tension that I hadn't known I'd been carrying left my body in one moment. Xander was gone. The man who had been hanging over my head as my fiancé for what felt like ages was no longer a threat, never able to steal me back again.

I burst into tears, and Hailey got up to hug me more gently this time.

"I don't know if I'm happy or relieved or upset at all the time he took away from me," I sobbed.

"You can be all of those at the same time."

The curtain parted, revealing the healer. "I'm sorry, Hailey, but Ruler Dexter is insisting on seeing Gisela alone. You'll be able to come back later."

"Okay." Hailey squeezed my hand. "You guys have a lot to talk about."

My heart pounded. "I know we do."

She let go of my hand and left. I gripped my pale blue blanket and took a steadying breath. Dex's familiar heavy footsteps got closer and closer until he was at the curtain. He paused, then pulled it back.

I anticipated being emotional, but I hadn't anticipated this. Dex's weariness triggered something inside of me, the desire to comfort him and pull him close. When he saw that I was okay, the weariness lifted into joy and, if I wasn't mistaken, love.

"Gisela," he said, his voice rough, like he had just woken up.

"Dex."

He crossed the room in a single stride, then gently cupped the back of my neck, pressing a kiss to my forehead. Waves of relief passed through our mate bond.

"I'm so sorry," he mumbled against my skin. "I know that's not enough when I hurt you this badly, but I am."

I looked up at him. I had never seen him look so distraught, so pale. His stubble had grown out to the point where it was almost a beard, and I ran my hand along it.

"I'm sorry for not believing you. For not trusting you, even though you had done nothing to warrant that kind of reaction," he said, still holding my face in between his hands. "I should have let go of the past that was holding me back. Almost losing you made me realize that actually losing you would be like losing part of myself."

His voice was thick with emotion, and I blinked back tears. His remorse rippled through the bond, making his words even more sincere.

"Thank you," I whispered. Our faces were inches away from each other, and I was tempted to close the gap with a proper kiss. But I held back. "You see why I lied, then?"

"I do. I had no idea it was him, and if I'd had, I would have believed you in an instant. I nearly ripped Xander apart for how he talked about you." A flush of anger came across his neck. "But I should have believed you before. The fear in your eyes when Zach and Geoffrey arrived..."

I put a finger to his lips. "It's okay. You more than proved how much you care about me."

"I don't just care about you, Gisela. I love you."

Finally, he kissed me. Our lips fit perfectly together, just as they had the very first time we'd kissed. He tasted like citrus and mint, the familiar smell of his hair and skin welcoming me home.

I always thought my life would be bleak, empty of all of the joyous feelings rushing through me. Men like Dex—with integrity and a good heart—hadn't existed in my world. Now I had my mate, and we had the rest of our lives to live together.

The mixture of unconditional love, happiness, and a hint of lust nearly bowled me over.

"Wow, I'm going to need to get used to that," I said, breathing heavily. "Feeling what you feel."

"It'll be an adjustment for me, too." He pressed his forehead against mine. "I never thought I could feel like this. Love isn't enough to describe it. I'd do anything for you, Gisela."

"You already did that before we were mates," I said with a chuckle. "You put your life at risk and killed Xander."

Just saying Xander's name made my mouth taste sour. Dex frowned.

"I hate the way you feel when you say his name." He brushed my hair behind my ear. "So scared and angry."

"I know. It's going to take me a long time to get over that feeling," I said. "In my mind, he's always out there, trying to get me back and break me."

"He's never going to hurt you or anyone else again." He pressed his lips to my forehead. "I don't want you to think about him anymore. Not now when we're having this moment."

"I don't want to, either." I beamed up at him. "I only want you."

"I'll always be here for you."

24

DEX

Being away from Gisela, even though we were only a five-minute walk apart, was a visceral feeling. Like she had been tucked against my side for hours, then suddenly taken away, leaving the cool air to chill my skin.

But I had to leave. The healer was giving her extra treatments so she could fully heal, which was all I wanted. And I had a lot of business to attend to.

My pack and council had gotten medical treatment as well and were gathered in my largest conference room, talking. They went quiet when I entered, excitement on their faces. Many of them probably noticed my mate bond. It was something any magical being could feel, whether someone's mate was in the room or not.

"We might have won the battle, but we still have work to do," I said. "What's the status of the arrests in connection to the failed uprising?"

Ryland stood. "We were able to stop the chain reaction of attacks, and obviously, we stopped Xander and his pack from starting any uprisings there. But we're still making arrests of groups who were involved. It's going to take time since we have to gather evidence, but it's happening."

"Good." I sat down at the head of the table.

"And I've contacted High Ruler Cora," Kai said, appearing by my side. "She's on her way."

Shit. Her appearance was inevitable. This issue was moments away from spilling into a lot of different creatures' domains, and we had High Ruler Filip involved, too. I hoped she'd understand that things sometimes spiraled out of our control. At least we'd stopped it this time.

"Prepare the formal meeting room for her. When is she coming?" I asked.

"Later today. We have time." Kai tapped around on his tablet. "And we need to meet with Ilona about punishing Xander's pack. She's still in her region, so we can call her."

"Let's do it now." I didn't want to rush through all of this, but I wanted to be close to Gisela again. And being close to her with everything settled sounded even better. Her contentment flowed through our bond, settling my nerves.

Kai and I went into my office, where he connected me with Ilona. She was in a bright, modern room, with mountains far off through the windows in the background. She looked as worn down by the events of the past few days as I did, but her eyes had optimism in there as well.

"Hello, Dexter," she said. "I'm glad to see you made it home in one piece."

"I don't think I got a single scratch during that fight. Did you?"

"No." She laughed. "But Xander's pack took some serious hits. And as you know, Xander is dead."

"I'm very aware." Satisfaction rippled through me.

Ilona shrugged, as if me ripping him limb from limb was a foregone conclusion. "We're arresting the vast majority of his pack. They're getting life sentences, no opportunity to shift. The bigger project is finding out how much his message has spread across the country. We have to figure out something with the population boom to prevent people from being angry."

My meeting with Cora came to mind. "I'm speaking with High

Ruler Cora about this situation later. I can let you know how that goes. See if we come up with a viable solution."

"That would be great." Ilona looked to her right again. "I have to go. I'll talk to you later."

She hung up. Kai, who had been standing to the side, took the tablet I had been using back. "High Ruler Cora would like to meet with you now."

"Okay." I paused, reaching out through our bond to see how Gisela was feeling. She was just fine, but I wanted to see her anyway. "Let me check on Gisela again, then I'll clean up before I meet with Cora."

I went back home, where I found Gisela out of bed and standing up. Most of her bandages were smaller than before, like they'd healed her faster than she naturally could on her own. Good. I only wanted the best care for her.

"Perfect timing!" the healer warlock said. "My healing here is done, at least for now. All of her bandages are waterproof, but they should come off in a few days on their own."

Gisela thanked the healer and grinned at me, going up on her tiptoes to give me a kiss. An odd medicinal scent clung to her, hiding her natural fragrance.

"Do you want to shower?" I asked. "With me?"

"Yes," she responded with a smirk.

I walked her back to my bathroom, which had a seat in the shower. I helped her undress, then placed her in there while I got the water running. A flare of lust and hunger reverberated from her to me as she watched me undress, and I gave her a wicked smile.

"Sorry," she said, putting her hands over her face. "You totally felt that."

"Why would you apologize?" I shut the clear shower door and took the shower head attachment off the wall. "I'm sure you felt how much I wanted you when I was taking your clothes off."

"I did." She looked up at me as I got her feet wet, then brought the water up over the rest of her body.

She tilted her head back as I wet her hair, letting out a warm hum of pleasure. I stopped her when she tried to move.

"Let me take care of you," I said. "It's the least I can do."

"You've already done so much," she replied, but she didn't protest.

I adjusted her body so I could sit behind her on the bench and start washing her hair. I massaged shampoo, then conditioner into her newly strawberry blonde hair, all the tension in her body melting away. Then, I moved down her body, carefully soaping up every inch of her soft skin. I missed her scent and how neatly she fit with me.

Every shift in emotions Gisela had, I felt, my body relaxing along with hers or flickering with arousal when I washed her breasts or between her thighs. If I spent too much time on those areas, I'd get swept up in her for the rest of the day, so I moved on.

"Is everything okay now?" Gisela asked after I rinsed soap off her legs. "With the uprisings and attacks?"

"Yes, it's all okay. We're making a lot of arrests," I added. "But it doesn't take away the bigger problem of territory issues." She felt the tinge of insecurity inside of me, so it was stupid to try to hide it. "I'm not sure what to do," I finally said. "I'm meeting High Ruler Cora later to debrief her. I have a few ideas, but they're ambitious."

"What ideas?"

"Restructuring all of the pack lands for all the beings across the region," I said. Gisela blinked. "Yeah, I know."

"Just bring up the idea. It has to be worth mentioning," she said. "Because clearly, it's an issue that could have led to a lot of death and destruction."

"True." Sharing something with her was a relief. I could tell she sincerely believed in me. "I'll try it."

"You'll do great. You're an amazing Ruler, and I'm not just saying that because you're my mate." The way her smile turned almost goofy when she said 'mate' tugged at my heart.

"Thank you, beautiful." I leaned down and kissed her. "Just know that I'll do whatever it takes to make the world safer and better for you, okay? Even if it's the harder road."

"I know. I believe you. And believe *in* you." She reached for my hand and gave it a squeeze.

Seeing her sitting there naked, water dripping all over her body, made me want to make this more than just a normal shower, but I restrained myself. Later. We had later and the rest of our lives. I finished rinsing her off, then showered myself, scrubbing off the dirt and soot off my skin. After, I put Gisela in one of my t-shirts and into bed with a stack of books.

"Good luck at your meeting," she said as I pulled on a nice button-down shirt.

"Thanks, I'll need it."

After I was fully dressed, I kissed her goodbye and went back to my headquarters. Kai had prepared the more formal meeting room. High Ruler Cora was already there, looking out the window with a cup of tea in hand. She was tall and elegant, the exact kind of person you'd assume was a leader. She was in a sleek pink dress that looked bright against her deep brown skin, and high heels that made her a few inches above six feet tall.

"High Ruler," I said, bowing my head.

"Hello, Dexter." She sized me up. "New mate?"

"Yes. Someone from Xander's pack." I pulled out her chair for her. "Her name is Gisela."

"Congratulations. This Xander fellow has thrown a serious wrench into a lot of Rulers' and High Rulers' plans." She sat down, and I sat down adjacent to her.

"He has. We've started the work of quelling any cells of criminal activities, but it's not a good solution to the problem. I've done every-thing I can to send additional resources to the fastest growing packs, but it's not enough."

Cora took my words in, nodding as if she wanted me to go ahead.

"I know it's a big task, but I believe we should redraw pack maps for all of the beings in the region," I said. "I know it's a lot just to avoid the dragons from fighting and trying to take over, but it's necessary at this point. This could have blown up into a full-fledged war."

She crossed one leg over the other. "So, you want to redraw the maps for everyone? Give everyone the proper amount of space all at the same time?"

"Exactly."

"That's a big project," she said.

"I know, but in the long run, it could be the best way to keep the peace across the region."

She considered my words, not taking her eyes off of my face. Her dark gaze was unnerving, especially since very few people ever made eye contact with me.

"I think you're right," she said. "We narrowly escaped disaster with this. Are you willing to be a part of the task force to tackle it?"

"Of course."

"Then we'll plan to meet to discuss the first steps soon." She looked to Kai, who came over. "Schedule a meeting with my aide, please. We'll have to clear a lot of calendar time."

"I'm on it."

Cora sipped her tea and put it on the table, once again giving me one of her long looks. "Can I give you some advice, Dexter? Now that you have a mate?"

"Sure, go ahead."

"If you keep her at the center of your decision-making—like the dragon shifters in your region are related to her—then you won't go wrong," she said. Her features softened. She had a mate, too, another mountain lion shifter named Liam.

"I'll take that to heart."

"Good. I think the future for dragon shifters will be bright."

With Gisela by my side, it was going to be. I was going to keep her safe no matter what, and I'd do anything to keep that promise.

EPILOGUE
GISELA

A year and a half later

"Oh, gods, Hailey, what is going on?" I demanded. I played along when she came to me this morning with a blindfold, but she had been walking me around the area near Dex and I's house with her hands on my shoulders for at least fifteen minutes.

"I can't spoil the surprise!" Hailey laughed.

"My feet ache. And my back aches! And the baby is sitting on my bladder!" I said.

For once, I was jealous of human women and their nine-month long pregnancy. I still had three months to go, and I was almost over it. I wanted to see our baby.

Dex and I found out we were pregnant nine months ago. We hadn't expected it to happen this soon, though we wanted a child at some point. I smiled at the memory of how shocked we were and how Dex immediately went into protective mode over me. Well, more protective than usual. He was going to be such a good father.

"We're almost there." Hailey squeezed my shoulders. "And here we are! Wait, keep the blindfold on."

I lightly stamped my foot in frustration, making her laugh. The room was full, wherever we were. The shuffling of feet and murmurs made me wonder how silly I looked in my cozy maternity dress, my hair up in a bun.

"Okay, you can take it off!" Hailey said.

I pulled it off and gasped. All of our friends were standing in a courtyard tucked toward the back of the headquarters compound, a party set up around them. Pink, blue, and yellow balloons and decorations were everywhere. We wanted to wait to see if we were having a boy or a girl, so I was happy to see Hailey had reflected that. Not that she'd do anything less. She was my best friend for a reason.

And most importantly, I was happy to see Dex, who was at the center of it all. We couldn't do real surprises since we felt each other's closeness or distance, but it didn't matter. Just seeing him when I wasn't expecting to was more than enough.

"I thought you were in meetings all day!" I rushed up to him and pulled him down for a kiss.

"This was the meeting." He shot Hailey a look, the corner of his mouth creeping up. "It was extremely important, according to Hailey. And it is."

"Even with all of the negotiations?" I asked.

News of redrawing all of the pack territory lines to give everyone adequate space had gone over extremely well, even though it was incredibly time intensive to buy, sell, or trade land that belonged to various packs and different kinds of beings. After making all of the arrests of people who wanted to take over other packs or other beings, it was a lot easier to spread the idea of diplomacy and peace, making everyone more amenable to the work that had to go into creating new territory lines. Dex was tied up for months trying to replace the Alphas who had been arrested for conspiring with others, but things had calmed down.

"Yep." Dex put his arm around my shoulder and rested his other hand on my belly. "Now we get to do whatever things Hailey planned for this."

"Cake first! Then gifts and games." Hailey clapped her hands together. "Come on, sit down, you two!"

She sat me down at the head of the table, where all of the friends I'd made were sitting there with smiles on their faces: Simeon and his mate Elyse, of course, people I had met during Dex's many dinners and meetings, friends that Hailey had introduced me to, and more. Now that Xander was dead and nearly all of the men in my old pack were, too, I felt so free. It made me happier around people and more open to talking. People out here could be trusted with time.

Hailey cut the cake, which was pink, blue, and yellow on the inside, and passed around slices. Dex fed me a bite first. It was so nice being open about our relationship. I thought people would judge me for it, but once again, I was pleasantly surprised. Even though I no longer worked in the kitchen, I was still friends with several people who did.

The rest of the baby shower was perfect. Alphas who were aligned with Dex had sent gifts, as had High Ruler Filip. His over-the-top baby toys probably cost so much that they'd make me sweat, but we appreciated the thought. Our closer friends, like Simeon and Elyse, got us more personal gifts that we were going to cherish forever: hand-embroidered baby blankets, adorable stuffed dragons, and more practical things like onesies for the baby to wear every day.

"Today was amazing, Hailey," I said after we saw off our final guests. "Thank you."

"Anything for you two." She smiled and gave me a hug, then Dex. "Someone else will lug all these gifts back to your house."

"Good, because I'm tired," I said with a yawn.

"Do you want me to carry you back?" Dex asked before scooping me up anyway.

"Well, I don't have a choice, do I?" I laughed, putting my arms around him.

He kissed the top of my head and carried me back to our home. I relaxed in his arms, feeling so safe and so free. Dex would have done anything to protect me and our child, and knowing that meant the world.

***

Discover more secrets of the Eternity Shifters in book six.

Savior or tormentor? The jury is out about the dragon shifter holding me prisoner.

I'm an orphan who hails from a dragon shifter pack that treats women like objects. I'm used to fending for myself.

However, I wasn't prepared to spend my life locked up for a crime I didn't commit.

My accuser is a High Ruler—a god among our kind. From his taut, muscular form to how he demands respect, he's an alpha to the core. The tension between us is palpable.

I want him in my bed as much as I want to destroy him.

Download Abandoned Dragon: Eternity Shifters Book Six

OTHER BOOKS YOU WILL LOVE

Veiled Realm: Complete Series Romance Collection
The rulers of the Veiled Realm are powerful, drop-dead gorgeous,
and lethal if you threaten their mates.

Fated Shifters: Romance Collection
True Mates. Secret Babies. Fake Relationships.
A shifter collection full of skin-tingling romances that are sexy,
suspenseful, and action-packed!

**Love, Lies and Billionaires: Complete Contemporary Romance
Collection**
Smoking Hot. Damaged. Forbidden.
Take a wild, toe-curling ride with these eight, full-length novels…